POP-UP TRUCK AND PERIL

A PINK CUPCAKE MYSTERY BOOK 5

HARPER LIN

ISBN-13: 978-1987859492

ISBN-10: 1987859499

www.harperlin.com

AMELIA HARLEY PULLED at the hangnail on her thumb as she sat on the couch in her living room with the telephone pinched between her right ear and shoulder.

"I don't know, Christine." She hemmed. "I can't say I'm jealous John is getting married. But it does feel weird. It's like some young, beautiful, bubble-headed thief has come and stolen my favorite coffee cup or my garbage-can lids. Those are certainly replaceable things, right? Things I could even live without. But totally inconvenient to lose."

"So you aren't going to the wedding?" Christine asked. Amelia heard her take a sip of wine, prompting her to do the same.

"I wasn't invited," Amelia stated.

"What?" Christine coughed as her wine went down the wrong pipe.

"It's okay. Really. It saved me from coming up with a reason not to go. Not to mention that now I don't have to buy a gift."

Amelia could hear Christine clicking her tongue. "I don't think that was John's idea. Was it?" Christine asked.

"I don't think so, but John did say he thought it would be for the best. He didn't want there to be any scenes at the ceremony or the reception." Amelia chuckled.

Christine laughed too. "He said that because he doesn't trust *her* not to make a scene," she said. "You are a class act. You'd never embarrass yourself or the kids that way. What a piece of work she is. She helped break up a marriage, but she doesn't think the ex-wife—the mother of her stepchildren—will remain composed enough at the party? You haven't been cyber-stalking her or literally stalking her without telling me, have you? She doesn't have *reason* to think you'd start throwing dishes, right?"

"No. What kind of person do you think I am? I don't stalk people. But, you might be right about the rest." Amelia took another sip of wine. The fruity pinot grigio was cold, yet it warmed her gut when she swallowed it.

"I know I am. What's her name?"

"Jennifer." Amelia sighed again.

"Yeah." Christine didn't hide her distaste. "Well, the best part of the ceremony will be Adam and Meg. I hate to say it, but it was really nice of John to make Adam his best man. That's a big deal for a seventeen-year-old boy and a nice way for them to get some father/son bonding."

Amelia nodded, switching the phone from her right side to her left. "It was."

"Is Meg doing anything?"

"Thankfully, no. She said she really didn't want to. I think the whole stepmom thing has her a little uneasy. Nervous. Like she has to do something different, instead of just being her wonderful self." Amelia bit her tongue to keep the tears back. But one of the reasons Christine was her dearest friend was because she could pick up on Amelia's feelings as if she were Jimmy-John's delivery—freaky fast.

"Amelia, don't do that." Christine tried to soothe her friend.

"Do what?"

"Blame yourself."

"It isn't that. I just hate to think the kids are

burdened or unsure or still hurting because of what John and I have done." Amelia sniffed and rubbed her nose with the back of her hand.

"Look, John is a piece of trash for what he did, and Jennifer will learn her lesson the hard way. But one thing I never saw was any neglect of the kids. You guys come together when it comes to them. That is the best you can hope for."

"Yeah. But a stepmom? Even I'm a little freaked out by it," Amelia admitted.

"Sure. It'll take some time, like easing into a new pair of shoes. It'll pinch for a while, but soon enough you'll break them in with repeated bending, flexing, and relentless pressure."

Amelia laughed.

"And let's face it. Step*mom*? More like a step-cheerleader or maybe a step-babysitter. Right? She's all of eighteen years old. Four years older than your beautiful daughter, who has proven to be mature beyond her years. I suppose Jennifer can certainly help Meg with applying mascara or painting her toenails."

"Jennifer is twenty-five," Amelia said, squealing in between her giggles.

"Oh." Amelia could hear Christine's eyes roll. "I stand corrected. She's got so much more to offer.

How to sneak into bars when you're underage? How to behave at a frat party."

"Christine, you are terrible." Amelia chortled. "You left out how to steal another woman's husband."

"I *thought* it, but didn't think I should *say it out loud*. Someday I'm going to have to answer for all my snide remarks and idle gossip." She cleared her throat. "I think I better get off the phone. You're a bad influence, Amelia. That's why you're my BFF."

"Right?" Amelia smiled, thankful her eyes were drying. "Well, as much as I hate to, I have to go, too. I've got to get ready for work on Monday."

"But it's only Friday. Girl, that Pink Cupcake *must* be working out for you," Christine said. "I promise I'm going to get my behind over there to Food Truck Alley and check things out. I'm such a loser. I haven't been there in forever."

"It's okay," Amelia chirped. "Life has a way of taking up all our time. I'll give you a call next week and we'll see if we can't pencil something in."

"That sounds great. Love to the kids." Christine rattled off a few more silly comments to leave Amelia laughing on the other end of the phone before they both hung up.

Amelia tossed the phone on the couch with one

hand and took another sip of the wine she was holding in her other hand. Listening to the quiet in the house, she wondered if this was how she was going to spend the rest of her days once the kids were grown and moved out.

As it was, they were with their dad and future stepmom for the weekend. From what John had said, it was really a weekend just with him, since Jennifer was so busy planning the wedding. They'd be going to the movies tonight then on a nature hike tomorrow, and in between they'd fill themselves with their favorite meals of pizza or Chinese food or burgers or whatever gooey, greasy, gassy meal their hearts desired.

The thought of them eating with their father, laughing and talking and telling him about their teenage dramas, made Amelia smile. But adding Jennifer to the mix soured the whole image.

"No use dwelling on it, Amelia," she scolded herself while getting up off the couch. "It is what it is."

With a deep breath, she went to her favorite room in the house, the kitchen. After taking another sip of wine, she decided she was ready to come up with a new cupcake, which would be a sugary-salty delight. How she'd get to that she wasn't sure, but that was the goal.

The regular double-chocolate decadence and peanut-butter-and-jelly cupcakes were selling faster than Amelia could bake them. But part of what made the Pink Cupcake, her food truck, a success was the unique flavor combinations she invented. She had salty flavors. She certainly had sweet flavors. The combination of both would be a delightful challenge.

It never failed that Amelia's mood always improved when she started to bake. Talking with Christine always helped, especially after the whole incident with Timothy Casey. She couldn't help her imagination running wild with images of him standing at the front door as she was about to leave or appearing at the garage door just as it was slowly rolling up.

It wouldn't happen. It couldn't happen. *But what if*, her mind kept asking. What if she hadn't gotten to the kids on time? Adam and Meg had no idea this man had committed murder before. They just got a real scare and a lesson on stranger danger. It wasn't them waking up in the middle of the night and coming to her room, asking to sleep in her bed after a nightmare. It was Amelia going to their rooms to make sure they were still there and that they were safe.

She took another sip of wine and then walked over to the pantry for some inspiration. When she slipped into her creativity cap, it didn't take long for the worries of Timothy Casey to remove themselves from the front of her mind, like the details of a horror movie melting away in a brightly lit room.

"Dark chocolate," she whispered. She pulled a box of Ghirardelli dark chocolate from the back of the cupboard. "What could be the oddest thing to go with this?"

The pantry door closed with a quiet snap. Amelia walked over to the fridge. As she gripped the handle, she made up a game in her head.

"The first thing your eye lands on will be the second main ingredient." It was the wine talking, for sure. If she managed to gaze upon the sliced avocado that was waiting to become guacamole or, worse, the skirt steak that was defrosting for beef and broccoli tomorrow, she'd just throw up her hands, hit the shower, and go to bed. But as she gave the door a tug and the little light blinked on, her eyes opened to a packet of hickory-smoked bacon.

"Oh, honey!" Amelia squealed. "We are gonna have some fun tonight!"

This was going to be an all-or-nothing cupcake. There was no holding back. A chocolate cupcake with bacon would be sweet and salty at the same time. She'd even add some sea salt. Definitely sea salt.

As Amelia waited for the cupcakes to bake, she managed to make guacamole, find the bag of chips she had hidden from the kids, and steam two frozen tamales on the stove.

After she ate, as she poured herself another glass of wine, the phone rang again.

"Hello, gorgeous," came the voice of Detective Dan Walishovsky.

"Well, hello, detective," Amelia replied, gushing. She wasn't as loopy since she had finally put some food in her stomach, but she could tell the two glasses of wine had definitely relaxed her. Plus, the voice on the other end of the phone always made her feel a little bit like a teenager. "Have I got a creation for you."

"Have you been baking?" he asked. Amelia and Dan had met during the course of a murder investigation. She wasn't sure what the motives of this tall, handsome, gray-eyed flatfoot were at first. But she had come to realize that he was more than just a guy with a badge. He was wonderful.

"I have. Tell me what you think of this: dark chocolate and bacon." Amelia rocked back on her heels.

"I think I'll be right over," he replied.

"Sounds great." Amelia's smile could be heard in her voice. She loved the time alone to enjoy the house and watch what she wanted on television without interruption. But having a grown-up visitor with grown-up manners and the ability to have grown-up conversation was a rare occurrence, one that Amelia welcomed.

CHAPTER TWO

WHEN SUNDAY FINALLY ARRIVED, Amelia anxiously waited for the front door to burst open and her kids to come filing in, dropping their backpacks on the floor and making a dash for the fridge. As teenagers, they were always hungry. Waiting on the counter for them were four of her new cupcake creations. Before she'd dare make them for the public, she wanted the approval of the Pink Cupcake's harshest critics.

They were right on time.

"Hi, Mom!" Meg yelled loud enough to reach the very edge of the backyard property line.

"Mom! We're home!" Adam boomed, not to be outdone by his sister.

"Yikes!" Amelia gasped, covering her ears with her hands. "I'm right here."

Meg skipped over and gave her mother a hug and a kiss. Adam, getting too big for hugs, just gave his mom a kiss on the top of the head. Amelia was sure it was to remind her how much taller he was than she. At seventeen Adam was almost six feet tall.

"I've got something for you guys to try." She scooted the plate over and watched their expressions.

Both children eagerly snatched up a cupcake, and each took a bite.

"Is there bacon in this?" Adam mumbled, letting a few crumbs escape and fall to the floor.

Nodding, Amelia smiled.

"It's crunchy and salty, yet smooth and choco-laty. Mom, this is your greatest creation so far!" Meg held up her hand in front of her mouth while she spoke. "It's like a breakfast dessert."

"Well, I was wondering what to call it." Amelia snapped her fingers. "Breakfast Dessert is the perfect name."

Meg beamed and looked up at her big brother, who nodded his head, too.

"Did you guys have fun at your dad's?"

They both looked at each other, putting that unspoken communication between siblings on full display.

"What is it?" Amelia asked.

"The wedding, Mom." Meg said after swallowing her mouthful of cupcake. "If I have to hear any more about that wedding, I'm going to barf."

"Oh, come on." Amelia patted her daughter's shoulder. "Jennifer is just excited. It's her first one," Amelia said sarcastically. That little voice inside her head laughed out loud. *It won't be her last. You can bet on it. If he'll do it* with *you, he'll do it* to *you.* But she kept her elaboration to herself.

"But Mom, she just won't stop. The bridesmaid dresses are gold lamé." Meg wrinkled her nose.

"No."

"They are, Mom," Adam said. "We saw pictures. Dozens of them." Adam sighed and grabbed his second Breakfast Dessert cupcake.

"Gold lamé? That's shiny stuff. Are you sure they aren't just a gold color?"

"Yes," the kids said in unison.

"Well, it's her big day. Who are we to tell her what's pretty? She has her own ideas, and maybe since she was a little girl she's always wanted a gold-themed wedding." *Perfect for a gold-digger.* Again,

Amelia kept her sarcasm to herself. "What does your dad say?"

"Nothing," they said together. Amelia looked from Adam to Meg and back again, wondering if they had practiced this.

"Well, Adam. Did you see the tuxes you and your dad would be wearing? Please don't tell me those are gold lamé, too." Amelia chuckled.

"Yeah, they're okay, I guess." He had finished the second cupcake in three bites.

"Don't you like them?"

"They are made for old men." Adam shook his head. "I look like the Penguin from those old *Batman* episodes Dan likes to watch."

Dan had spent one evening enlightening the kids regarding the old Adam West *Batman* series, making them laugh as he read the comic words like *pizzzow* and *thurrrump*. In one of the episodes, the Caped Crusader fought Burgess Meredith, who Dan said played the best version of the Penguin out of all the different versions of the DC Comics villain. Amelia couldn't help but laugh at her son's description. "Do you have a top hat and tails?" she asked.

"Yes. They are all black and gray and white. I look ridiculous."

Amelia stood up and smoothed her son's wildly curly hair away from his forehead.

"Well, just remember that once the reception starts, you can dump the jacket and the hat, and you'll have lots of fun dancing and talking and eating. Trust me, you'll have a great time."

Amelia couldn't help but feel a little vindicated that her children were not all that impressed with Jennifer's tastes. But it made sense. She was only a couple years older than they were. Tacky and gaudy were still acceptable traits for a woman in her early twenties to have. But it did make Amelia wonder what the wedding dress looked like. She made a mental note to call Christine and tell her all about it.

As it turned out, the following day, as soon as the Pink Cupcake opened for business, Amelia received a desperate call from Christine. It wasn't the normal desperate, with the kids acting up or her husband stapling his thumb to his forefinger. This was on a completely different level. She was terrified.

"Calm down, honey. Breathe," Amelia said

soothingly into her cell phone. "Now, what did you say happened?"

"Danielle Wilcox. She was the secretary for us in the Marketing Department." Christine huffed like she'd run up eight flights of stairs.

"I met her, right? Pretty girl who wore her hair in a beehive."

"Yes. That's her. She'd been here for a little less than a year." Christine blubbered. "She's dead. Murdered. They found her stabbed in the supply room."

Amelia gasped. "What? You're kidding." Her left hand latched on to Lila, her assistant at the food truck, and her eyes gaped. "Murdered?"

CHAPTER THREE

"YES. My gosh. Of course. Come on over. Do you remember where the truck is?" Amelia nodded. "Yes. That's right. Drive carefully, and I'll see you in a little bit."

Amelia looked at Lila and shook her head before letting go of her arm. She'd hired Lila Bergman to handle the accounting for the Pink Cupcake, but she turned out to be a wonderfully unique woman who loved the business as much as Amelia did. It took her about one day not only to earn Amelia's trust, but to become a good friend.

"Did you just say 'murdered'?" Lila asked, pushing her flaming-red hair away from her face with the back of her hand. "Who was murdered?"

"That was my friend Christine. She works at the

Master Ketchup factory, over in the Pilfer neighborhood. You know, where all those industrial areas are?" Amelia watched Lila nod. "Christine works in the marketing department and said they found the secretary there murdered."

Lila balked. "What is the world coming to? How do they expect to keep people on board when secretaries are getting murdered? No wonder no one stays at a job long these days."

"Lila." Amelia stifled a chuckle. "I'm sorry. This is no laughing matter."

"You're right." Lila finished preparing the batter for twenty-four orange-vanilla cupcakes that would taste, amazingly, like Dreamsicles. "Do you know what happened?"

"No. But they are letting the staff go home and shutting everything down for the day while the police investigate," Amelia said, absently dropping the paper cups into the cupcake tin. "Christine is on her way over here to tell me what she knows."

Amelia guessed her friend had begged the bus driver to break the speed limit and blow a few red lights to make it to Food Truck Alley as quickly as she did. From a distance, Amelia recognized the woman in a black pencil skirt and pink dress shirt, who waved as she approached the truck. Amelia approached her friend to find Christine's eyes red with tears.

"You poor thing." Amelia hugged Christine tightly then led her to the back of the truck and up the steps to take a seat. "Christine, you remember Lila. She helps me run this beast."

After a quick smile and a hug for Lila, Christine began to tell them both what had happened when she arrived to work.

"It was a typical Monday morning," she began. She had gotten off the number twenty-two bus right on the corner of Hatter Avenue and Lint Street. The Master Ketchup Factory was a long brick building that took up an entire city block. For many years, it had been a dingy gray color, but when the grandfather who had started the business retired, the son, Regis Master, decided to update the facility. That included updating the assembly line, installing state-of-the-art robotics in some areas, utilizing cutting-edge software for the office, jump-starting the marketing efforts, and painting a mural of a lush, fruitful tomato garden across the front of the building.

Decorative stone planters were placed at the entrance, which grew beautiful flowers every season. It was like a garden oasis in the middle of a steel-and-brick wasteland.

With the marketing department expanding, Christine had gotten a job there over seven years ago and had no plans on leaving. At least not until now.

"I said goodbye to Danielle on Friday," she said, taking a sip of coffee from a Styrofoam cup, her hands trembling slightly. "She had gotten a late delivery of supplies that she was stacking in the supply closet. That's where they found her this morning with… her throat slit."

Lila gasped. "Oh my gosh."

"How long had Danielle worked there?" Amelia asked as she mixed the batter for her airy, whipped-vanilla frosting.

"She had just had her six-month review and had passed with flying colors." Christine looked into her coffee as if she were reading her fortune at the bottom. "I should know, because I did part of the review myself. She was so creative. Simple things she'd suggest had huge impacts on design and word concepts. Press releases were exciting and enter-taining when she wrote them. She had a knack, and I couldn't wait until she had made her one-year mark, because I was going to request she be my marketing coordinator."

"I have to ask this, because I'm morbid," Lila interrupted. "Did you see the body?"

"Thank heavens, no." Christine's eyes bugged from their sockets. "I would have totally tossed the rye toast and orange juice that I had for breakfast this morning."

"What did the police have to say?" Amelia asked, hoping to hear Dan's name in the mix. It would make things so much easier to find out if he was involved.

"I have no idea. We were all held in the lobby. No one was allowed to go to their offices. Regis came and made an announcement that the shop was going to be closed, all departments, for the entire day, but that we'd still get paid, yadda, yadda. It wasn't until he said counselors would be made available to anyone who was traumatized by the incident that it really hit home what had happened." Christine stared at the cupcakes, but it was obvious she didn't really see them. They were just the things that were in her field of vision.

"You know, I hate to nitpick, but are counselors really necessary?" Lila asked. Amelia knew her friend was not trying to be disrespectful. It was just that it never occurred to Lila that some people might have nightmares knowing a person was killed at their place of employment. In Lila's mind, if *you* were having nightmares, it meant the bad guy didn't get you.

"I don't know," Christine replied, pulling her lips down at the corners. "I'm *here* for my therapy. But I'll tell you what. I'm going to go home and tell the old man and the kids about this, and they are going to want to know every gory detail even if I have to make stuff up."

Amelia laughed and was happy to see a smile on Christine's face. "That's good, though. Don't keep something like this from them," Amelia said, encouraging her friend.

"I can't, even if I wanted to. Danielle was my assistant. What if this loony has it out for the whole marketing department? What if I was the real target, or maybe Leana, who was the marketing director? I'm not sure what I should do. Maybe I shouldn't even go back."

"You love that job." Amelia watched her friend's eyes tear up.

"Yeah, but not enough to die for it." She chuckled, wiping a tear from her cheek.

"There are no jobs worth dying for," Lila

added. "Sorry, Amelia. I love you. I love the kids. I love the Pink Cupcake. But the day someone brandishes a knife and says, 'It's you or the truck,' I'm retiring."

Amelia and Christine both laughed. "You are absolutely right," Amelia said. "That will make two of us. So, do they have any suspects?"

"I have no idea. But I was wondering…" Christine looked at Amelia sheepishly. "What are you doing for the next five days?"

"What?" Amelia patted the back of her neck, smoothing her short hair. "I'm working. Why?"

"You wouldn't want to consider coming up to Pilfer by the factory to do a little snooping around on your own?"

"Are you crazy?" Amelia looked at Lila and then back to Christine. "After the close call I had last time with a crackpot showing up at my front door when the kids were alone, I think my private-detective hobby is pretty much over."

"Please?" Christine nearly begged. When Amelia looked at her, she didn't see the same girl she had known for so much of her life. This wasn't a request for Amelia to find out the gory details and relay them back, something Christine might have asked her to do at one time. This was something else completely. "Jason is going to be out of town. Perfect timing, right? If you had the truck parked there, no one would suspect anything odd, and you could, well, make sure I got on and off the bus safely. I know it's a lot to ask, but…"

"You're that scared?" Amelia took her friend's hand in her own.

"My gut just says I shouldn't let my guard down."

"What do you think, Lila? A little change of scenery might be nice?" Amelia looked at Lila, who shrugged her shoulders.

"I'm game if you are." Lila blinked, trying not to look excited about the whole adventure, even though she was, and Amelia knew it.

"You met a good number of these people already," Christine pleaded. "At Denise's barbeques and Christmas parties, a lot of them showed up. You won't be around complete strangers."

The idea of seeing Denise Giordano sent ripples of annoyance up Amelia's spine. She had been a good friend of Amelia's at one time. At least, that was what Amelia thought, until it was discovered that Denise knew all about John's affair with Jennifer for months before she said anything to Amelia. It seemed everyone knew about John's infidelity before Amelia did. That was something Amelia could eventually forgive but never forget. She had yet to do either of these things with Denise. "Lord, please tell me Denise and the rest of the girls aren't going to be loitering around there. When was the last time you saw them?"

"I haven't seen Denise since the last time you made me cozy up to her to milk her for information. I'm not a fair-weather friend, Amelia. You know that."

Amelia looked at Christine and remembered how many times she had cried on Christine's shoulder after the divorce was still fresh and her heart was raw. When Amelia needed her, she was there with no questions asked. It was time to return the favor.

"All right. It will require a little quick paperwork, but there shouldn't be a problem getting a permit for the street." Amelia looked at Lila.

"I've made a friend at City Hall." Lila winked. "Let me give him a call and see what he can do. I'm sure there are people who've asked for bigger favors than this." She chuckled out loud, only to see both Amelia and Christine looking at her suspiciously.

"A new friend?" Amelia looked at Christine and then back to Lila, who was blushing. "You didn't tell me you made a new friend, and in City Hall, no less."

"A woman should always have a few secrets." Lila moved the cooled cupcakes, placing them on the rack at the service window. Before long, they were all gone and being replaced by a concoction of double chocolate and raspberry that Amelia had given to Christine on the house to help soothe her nerves.

"Just stay as long as you like. In fact, why don't you relax, and I'll give you a lift home at five. You don't want to take the bus until you talk with Jason and he knows what's going on." Amelia wiped sweat from her forehead. "In fact, I'd suggest you go get yourself something solid to eat. Gavin next door makes a fantastic Philly cheesesteak. And there's the Charming Wok or the Turkey Club, too. Anything sound good?" Amelia couldn't stop her motherly instincts from coming out. She didn't care what the popular opinion was. Comfort food did exactly what it was supposed to do, and sometimes it was the best remedy to help you relax, get a good night's sleep, and see things anew in the morning.

Christine took her advice. By five o'clock, she had not only had lunch and talked all about the murder, but she had also filled Amelia in on her future plans to build a deck, get the kids their vaccinations for school, and her suspicions that her twenty-year-old niece was heading down the wrong path with a fellow with no job and no college, but a huge attitude.

She apologized. "My gosh, I don't think I've stopped talking since I got here."

"I think you are a little bit in shock," Amelia said. "Let's get you home. Maybe those counselors aren't such a bad idea." She pushed a lock of Christine's hair away from her face.

"I'll be all right." She let out a deep breath. "Do you really think you can be on the street outside the factory tomorrow?"

"If I know Lila, I could probably show up there right now and be welcomed by not just the Board of City Vendors, but the Teamsters and Department of Revenue, too." Amelia chuckled.

"I'll feel a lot better if you are." Christine nodded her head. "I know it sounds crazy."

"Believe me"—Amelia patted Christine's hand —"when I felt like the bottom fell out, you gave me the rope to grab hold of. That's sometimes all we need to feel better. It'll be fine."

Amelia watched the shadow of relief fall over Christine's face. It made Amelia feel a little strange though. Here was her friend, who lived in a house full of boys and faced challenge after challenge with them recreating the World Wrestling Federation in their backyard, experimenting with electricity, and pushing the boundaries of human hygiene to their limits, but this death had sent her into a tailspin.

Meanwhile, Amelia had been around several deaths that were gruesome in their own right. But even now she wasn't that shaken by them. Or had she been, and she just swallowed it down in order to keep going?

If I can live through my husband dumping me for a twenty-something, I can live through anything. She nodded to herself. It was true. That would be the last time she thought about Timothy Casey and his attempt to hurt her children. He didn't do it, and he never would. Being frozen like Christine just couldn't be part of Amelia's life. No matter what happened, she had to be strong for her kids, for Dan, for Lila, for the Pink Cupcake, and now for Christine.

CHAPTER FOUR

IT DIDN'T TAKE LONG for the hot-pink food truck to gain the attention of the employees at the Master Ketchup factory. As an extra bonus, Amelia also gained a few customers from Alco Gravure, the factory catty-corner from Master Ketchup, and from a couple of city workers who were repairing some of the potholes in the alleys in the area. Business-wise, coming to the Pilfer neighborhood was a goldmine.

"This will be the first time a murder got us *more* business," Lila pointed out.

"Right?" Amelia smiled as she pulled out her second batch of PB&J cupcakes. She didn't want to be flippant. After all, Danielle was someone's daughter. She was a good employee, and people knew her. Plus, she was about Jennifer's age, and that was too young to be dead. That thought held Amelia captive.

Just admit it. How many times did you think of murdering Jennifer and *John after you were served the divorce papers? There are a lot of women who'd say you were within your rights to temporarily lose your mind.*

It was true. A secretary and a boss? A jealous wife? It was an old, old story. One worth considering, especially since she had occupied the jealous-wife role and could have easily taken that short baby-step into complete lunacy. She hid her thoughts and smiled kindly to the burly man in a white T-shirt and neon-orange vest who had just ordered three PB&J cupcakes for himself.

"Well, this is an unexpected surprise."

Amelia heard the familiar voice and looked up to find Dan looking at her seriously. His partner, Eugene Gus, waved cheerfully to Amelia from behind the older detective.

Amelia could see in Dan's expression that he wasn't exactly thrilled she was there. "Hi guys. Have you had any breakfast? Can I get you guys a warm cupcake, some coffee, maybe?"

"No, thanks, Amelia," Eugene replied. "I'm trying to watch my weight." He patted his stomach and smiled. Unlike Dan, Eugene was soft around the middle.

"Eugene, why don't you get things started inside," Dan ordered without taking his eyes from Amelia.

"Amelia, I can handle the window. It's getting close to that first bell of the day." Lila patted Amelia's arm. "The crowd is already slowing down."

"Are you sure?"

"Yeah." Lila nodded and looked at Dan then back at Amelia.

"Thanks. I'll just be a minute." Amelia squeezed Lila's hand back and walked off the back of the truck, slowly approaching Dan. "You look so serious. Is everything okay?"

"Why aren't you at Food Truck Alley?" Dan inquired, as if he were questioning her whereabouts on the night Danielle Wilcox was killed.

"Well, funny story. You see, my dear friend Christine works here." Amelia took a deep breath. "This is the woman who spent several nights a week with me after the divorce, cheering me up, helping with the kids, basically holding me together with her bare hands. She's pretty shaken up about the whole murder thing and asked me to just come and keep my eyes and ears open through the day, and then to make sure she gets on the bus all right at five."

"Amelia, after what happened with Timothy Casey, do you really think this is a wise move?" Dan thrust his hands into his pockets and anxiously jingled his keys.

"Oh, Dan. Lightning doesn't strike twice in the same place." Amelia looked up at him and tried to convey with her eyes that she appreciated his concern but could take care of herself.

"We're not talking about lightning, Amelia." He put his hand on her shoulder and squeezed it gently. "We don't even really know what we're dealing with yet." He licked his lips and looked off behind her and down the street, focusing on nothing but seeing everything from the garbage cans next to the lamp posts, to the red fire plugs, to the graffiti scribbled along the brick walls of the neighboring warehouses and factories, to the ropy cracks in the sidewalk that led to Amelia's size-six shoes.

"I'm not playing Sherlock Holmes, Dan. I'm just here for a friend. For some reason, she feels safe with me around. If I see or hear anything, I promise to call you first." She crossed her chest with her hand and held up three fingers. "Scout's honor."

Finally, Dan's gray eyes softened, and a slight curl at the right corner of his lips finally made an appearance.

Amelia blushed a little and stepped into his personal space, straightened his tie, and brushed the lapels of his suit jacket smooth.

"That's a deal," Dan stated. "How long do you plan on being here?"

"Just for the week." Her eyes twinkled. "I'll bet my week's salary that nothing is going to happen. You'll probably go up there and find out the answers to everything in just a few minutes. I'd put my money on a scorned wife."

"What makes you say that?" Dan walked Amelia to the back of her truck and gently took her hand in his to help her up the steps.

"Because I was one, once." She rolled her eyes and smiled.

"Hey, Lila." Dan nodded at the other woman. "You're looking lovely today. Do me a favor, would you? Keep an eye on this one." He jerked his thumb in Amelia's direction. "I have the feeling that all of her best intentions will still lead her into trouble."

"I agree," Lila teased.

"Thanks a lot." Amelia went to the first oven and checked the time on the timer. "Like he needs any encouragement."

"You know, she just does it to impress you, Dan," Lila offered.

"I thought as much," Dan replied, smiling.

"You guys are horrible," Amelia mumbled.

Within a few seconds, Dan was heading into the Master Ketchup office to interview the staff.

CHAPTER FIVE

WORK WHISTLES WENT off around the neighborhood, and the streets became void of any pedestrians. The trucks that noisily rumbled by were all huge, heavy behemoths, rattling chains from their back bumpers or shaking like thunder as the empty trailers bounced over the massive potholes caused by so many big trucks cruising down the street.

A garbage truck lifted and overturned enormous dumpsters filled with everything from fast food lunch bags to bags of shredded, ten-year-old tax forms. Heavy scraps of wood, metal, and plastic cascaded noisily into the garbage truck's open maw and then were crushed under the pressure of the hydraulic press, which kicked in with a whine and shudder.

"For a place with so few people on the street, it is noisy out here." Lila scattered some flour on the clean cutting board, in preparation for creating her very first lavender petals made out of frosting. "There could be six people getting murdered down the block, and we wouldn't hear them if they were screaming… well… bloody murder."

"Well put," Amelia replied, chuckling and focusing on two mixers she had going simultaneously.

In Food Truck Alley, people visited the Pink Cupcake steadily throughout the day, but here, foot traffic just about stopped by eight o'clock. Just as the midday-break whistle shot through all the other noises in the area, Amelia placed the last batch of Dreamsicle cupcakes on the rack at the service window.

Just in time, too, as the employees of all the nearby factories and mills came spilling out of their buildings to enjoy a little fresh air or a cigarette, or to grab something to eat from one of the several food trucks parked along the way.

Amelia kept her eye on the people coming from Master Ketchup. It was quite a diverse group, to say the least. The murmurs and bits of conversation Amelia could overhear were of Danielle Wilcox and the murder. Some women were visibly shaken, wiping their eyes with crumpled-up tissues they'd probably been using all morning. Others nodded and gave sympathetic glances and pats on the back.

But there was one fellow who caught Amelia's attention. Leaning up against the brick wall by himself was this short guy who reminded Amelia of some of the boys she'd seen at Adam and Meg's school, strutting around in tight clothes to show off their physique, striking poses leaning against the gym walls, and acting as if they were really too good to be with the rest of the crowd.

In reality, the crowd usually found them too obnoxious to be around. Fascinated, Amelia studied him as he smoked a cigarette, and she saw him roll his eyes at more than one female who walked by, dabbing her eyes or crying outright. Another guy joined him. This new guy was at least a foot taller and wore glasses. The half-pint changed his attitude. He became animated, laughing, smiling, shrugging his shoulders, and cracking jokes that only he laughed at.

Not normal, Amelia thought. Like some men who suffer a Napoleon Complex due to their height, this guy was determined to make himself known—even if it was by being as insufferable as possible.

"You suspect Shorty over there?" Lila whispered, adding a five and two tens to the register.

"Yeah, how did you know?"

"He stands out like a sore thumb. Doesn't look too broken up about this whole murder, either." Lila smiled at the next customer in line.

Amelia would describe him to Christine later. In the meantime, while Amelia knew Dan and Gene were still in the building taking statements and looking for surveillance-camera footage, here on the sidewalk, a very nervous guy in overalls made a dash across the street.

In between handling the cupcakes and putting them carefully into their hot-pink boats or tiny pastry boxes, she observed that there wasn't anything across the street except a car impound lot. It wasn't the kind of place that let people in to just roam around. In fact, there was a guard booth at the front with a rather large man with a frown on his face reading the paper inside.

Squinting, Amelia spotted the man in overalls as he jogged along the chain-link fence that kept all the booted cars safe during the off hours. He disappeared behind a Ford Taurus and the other brick building behind the fence.

For a second, Amelia wondered if she should

call Dan and let him know. For all she knew, the person was fleeing the scene. He could be the person responsible for murdering Danielle Wilcox, and she was letting him get away.

Could it really be that simple? Did the case already get solved? No—not until the guy is in cuffs and in the back of Dan's car.

She reached for her phone, and just as she was about to hit Dan's number on her speed dial, a woman in a tight black skirt and kitten heels walked, with her arms folded over her chest, in the same direction. Amelia shut her phone off and put it back in her pocket. "Well, that's interesting."

"What?" Lila wiped her forehead, leaving a streak of white powder behind like Indian war paint.

"Nothing. Just saw a couple slip off behind that building."

"A couple of what?" Lila asked, only half listening to Amelia.

"A couple. You know, a man and a woman." Amelia chortled.

"Oh." Lila smiled. "Eww. Love behind the auto pound. How romantic."

Amelia nodded, but she wasn't completely

convinced their behavior was love. Maybe she was just being paranoid.

"Excuse me!" a shrill voice called. "Excuse me. Do you work here?"

Amelia snapped out of her daydream and looked down from the service window. Staring up at her was a gargoyle from the spires of Notre Dame.

CHAPTER SIX

"YES, CAN I HELP YOU?" Amelia wasn't accustomed to people being rude to her, but as soon as she decided she didn't like this woman, who had a large, sparkling diamond wedding set on her ring finger and several of those Pandora bracelets jingling around her wrists, she remembered that *the customer is always right.* Quickly, she put on a smile.

"Are these made with cage-free eggs?"

Amelia almost started to laugh. *Yes, ma'am. The eggs were never placed in any cages. However, I do believe they were subjected to baskets.* "I'm sorry. These were made with eggs from the grocery store. I can't for certain say the chickens were cage-free."

Amelia was proud of herself for telling the truth. It gave her a twinge of satisfaction that the truth would probably make this miserable-looking woman stomp away.

But the enticing smell of sugary sweetness, the beautiful presentations and the continual "yums" and "wows" coming from the other new patrons seemed to be too much for this dame. She jumped from the moral high ground and ordered three Dreamsicles.

"I hope you enjoy them. I'll look into that cage-free business. It might be a good option for us," Amelia offered sincerely, smiling.

"Don't patronize me." The woman gave Amelia a quick smile, the kind of smile that said, *I've decided you're trash. You and your tacky pink truck and caged eggs.* "Animals have rights, too. They deserve them more than people do." Without allowing for a reply, the woman turned and elbowed her way back into the building.

"What in the world was that all about?" Lila stared at Amelia with wide eyes.

"You know, you just can't make some people happy." Amelia shook her head. "But you'll notice she took the cupcakes. Not too proud to eat the cupcakes. Sheesh."

Animals have rights, too. They deserve them more than people. Not a smart comment to make after a murder. But, unfortunately, it was a common mantra among many people in this day and age. It wasn't against the law to be weird.

Before Amelia had a chance to take a deep breath, a petite, mousy woman came running up to the window, her brown eyes bugging from their sockets and red around the edges. She ordered a Dreamsicle, a chocolate and raspberry, and one of the PB&J cupcakes, which Amelia served to her.

"Thank you." She sniffed, wiping her nose on the back of her sleeve and hurrying into the factory just as the whistle blew. Like Pavlov's dogs, everyone had been trained to know that whistle meant it was time to get back to work.

As if on cue, the woman in the tight-fitting black skirt came hustling back from across the street. She was smoothing her hair back and looking down as she tugged at the bottom of her blouse. A few seconds later, the man in the overalls made his appearance, heading back into the factory by way of another door off the alley.

Amelia turned and saw Christine, who looked tired. "How's it going?"

"I'm okay." She smoothed her hair out of her face. "Jason drove me in this morning. Like I predicted, he and the kids wanted to know all the gory details, but he's going to pick me up when he gets off work, so you don't need to drive me."

"I'll be happy to wait with you if you'd like. In fact, I've got a few questions for you about some of the characters I saw today."

"Sure. Sounds good. I've got to get back to work. I'll see you at lunchtime."

Christine waved and said goodbye to Lila then disappeared inside the factory.

"I don't know. There is something about this part of town that feels weird," Lila said. "Don't get me wrong, I like the business and, other than the free-range-chicken lady, everyone has been pleasant enough. It just feels weird."

"Maybe it is because a murder took place right in this building?" Amelia offered.

"No. It's sort of like an incestuous feeling."

"Good Lord, Lila. What kind of trashy novels have you been reading?" Amelia teased.

"Hear me out." Lila took a seat and grabbed a bottle of ice water for each of them. "The financial district and the shopping district are too far to walk to. There are no restaurants. There is a bar over there"—she pointed down the street to its south-western corner—"and another one behind us about two blocks. The only people these people see are the people who work here. There are no tourists, no out-of-towners, no other business people. It's like they are in a bowl."

Amelia nodded. Lila was absolutely right. If you were a single lady looking for romance or a man looking for opportunities, both options were pretty limited.

"So, what does it mean?" Amelia asked.

"I don't know. But the chances of an outsider roaming into this wasteland to bump off a secretary are pretty weak."

That made sense. The only problem was that even in this "incestuous" bubble of people, there were hundreds of possible suspects. Sure, Amelia picked a few weirdoes out of the bunch, but the chances of any of them being the actual slicer were pretty slim.

That's okay. She soothed herself. *You are here to make Christine feel safer. You don't have to solve this case. That is why Dan is here.*

But he had yet to come out of the building. Even after the lunchtime whistle blew, she hadn't seen him or Gene. No matter how hard she tried to control herself, she couldn't help thinking the jittery feeling would only be relieved once she talked to Dan.

But, with every passing hour, with each request for business cards and compliments on the cupcakes, there was still no sign of him. He wouldn't have just left without saying goodbye. Something had to be going on inside the building that was keeping him very busy.

"Hey, Lila. Before you pack up for the evening, let me run inside and use the bathroom." Amelia untied her apron and pulled it over her head.

"Sure," Lila said as she began to get the routine cleaning started before tackling the receipts.

Amelia walked to the entrance of the Master Ketchup and yanked open the door. The coolness of the air conditioning sent a shiver up her back. First, she scanned the lobby for the familiar man in the gray suit, but Dan was nowhere to be found.

"Can I help you?" A young woman with squinty eyes and heavy gloss on her lips stared at her.

"Yes." Amelia walked up to the semicircle reception desk. "I work at the Pink Cupcake food truck outside. The guys from the auto pound and the factory across the street staked their claim on the Porta Potties out there. Is there any way I can use your restroom?"

"We don't have a public restroom." She pulled

her shiny lips away from her teeth like she was ripping off a bandage.

"I know. But I wouldn't be asking if it wasn't kind of an emergency."

She pulled the keycard from behind the lip of her desk. "Can you make it quick? I'm not really supposed to do this."

"I'll be in and out." Amelia raised her hand as if she were taking a solemn oath. She took the key and followed the receptionist's directions, heading down the hallway, making a left before the water cooler, and then down to the white door with the little red tomato with eyelashes on the door.

"Cute." Amelia looked around and headed further down the hallway to what looked like a corral of cubicles.

"I don't care," a male voice said. Slowly, Amelia peeked around the corner and saw the angry half-pint she had witnessed smoking this morning. "She was a bitch."

"Aren't you even the least bit sad?" Another male voice could be heard, but Amelia could only see his shoes emerging from the cubicle he was sitting in. "I mean, there was a time you wanted to go out with her."

Half-Pint shrugged his shoulders and again

rolled his eyes. "Yeah. What a waste. I should have known she was just a tease."

"She wasn't a bad person, though. I thought she was kind of nice," the mystery man argued. "She was nice to me, anyways. Always smiling and laughing."

"Yeah. Well, she's not laughing now."

"I don't know, Lenny. It doesn't mean she deserved to be killed."

"Sometimes a man just gets pushed to his limits."

"It's 'pushed to his limit,' you knucklehead," Amelia whispered. Hearing footsteps behind her, she quickly turned around and pretended to be looking for the bathroom. Before anyone saw her, she tapped the keycard to the door handle and, as soon as the light turned green, she slipped inside. Peeking out the door, she saw the strange caged-egg woman stomp past. Thankfully, she didn't come in the bathroom. That was the last place Amelia wanted to run into her.

Taking advantage of the opportunity, Amelia stepped into the corner stall closest to the door, slipped the lock into place, took a seat, and pulled a pen from her pocket. On the palm of her hand she wrote the name "Lenny" so she wouldn't forget Half-Pint's real name.

Two women came into the bathroom. "I still can't believe it," one said, and Amelia instinctively pulled up her feet and held her breath as she heard the ladies checking for anyone else in the bathroom who might be listening.

"It had to be one of the guys from the warehouse."

"Why do you think that?"

"The way she'd go out there, she'd flirt with anything in pants. And you know as well as I do that some of those guys back there don't have the greatest reputations. What about Keith? He's got those spiderweb tattoos on his elbows. Those are prison tattoos. I know it. I saw that on *Cold Case Files*."

"Really?"

"Uh, yeah?"

"Why are you telling me this? I have to go out there three or four times a day to make sure my samples get sent."

"Yeah, but you're not out there shaking it and practically holding up a sign for the guys to notice you. I'm telling you, as sure as I'm standing here, it was one of those dudes from the warehouse. In the next couple of days, we'll get a memo that says so-and-so will no longer be working at Master Ketchup because he's a psycho who slashed Danielle's throat."

Amelia had propped herself up with one hand against the stall wall, with both feet up in the air. She tried to stretch her neck to get a look at an outfit or a pair of shoes through the tiny crack between the stall wall and the door, but there was nothing. She had no idea who the women were, or even a slight detail to identify them to Christine.

Without wasting any more time, she took a deep breath, emerged from the stall, and dashed to the door. Tightly, she gripped the handle and pulled the door open, only to find Dan and Gene coming from the direction of the cubicles.

"Oh, hey." She stroked the back of her neck and tilted her head to the right. "I had to use the ladies' room before the long ride home. You guys have a good day?"

"Let's just say we had a day." Dan slipped his hands into his pockets. "Gene, you go ahead to the car. I'll be there in a minute."

"Sure thing, Dan. G'night, Amelia."

"Have a nice night, Gene." Amelia liked Dan's partner. Sure, he was still green, at least compared to her favorite crusty old investigator, but she knew he had Dan's back. That was important to her. She looked up at Dan.

"What are you doing tonight?" he asked, his voice aching like a sore muscle.

"Well, I was going to make sure Christine's husband picked her up, and then I was just going home. Why? What have you got in mind?"

"Nothing but a couple of burgers at Moody's and a little conversation about anything but this case."

"It's not looking good, huh?"

Dan shook his head and clicked his tongue. "There are a lot of secrets in this place. I'm not sure what to make of it all, but with this many people and the possibility of a deliveryman or bike messenger thrown into the mix, it seems like a needle in a haystack. That's all I can say."

"You'll see it clearer after a burger and a good night's rest," Amelia said soothingly. "I better get going. I don't want to get the receptionist in trouble."

"That bubblehead? She's probably already forgotten you are here." Dan winked at her. "I'll meet you at your place. If the kids are around, we can take them with."

Amelia bounced on her toes. "They'd love that." She blew Dan a kiss and hurried to the reception area, where the receptionist was tearing apart her desk.

"Thanks again. Sorry I took so long." She handed the receptionist the bathroom key.

"Oh, you had it." She sighed. "I thought I had lost it. No problem. Have a good night."

Amelia almost started to giggle as she realized Dan was right.

CHAPTER SEVEN

AFTER A LIVELY DINNER of burgers and fries with her three favorite people, Amelia spent a few romantic minutes with Dan, standing outside his car as Meg and Adam waved goodbye and went into the house.

"What a day." Amelia yawned. "Will you be back at the Master Ketchup factory tomorrow?" She hadn't talked to him about the murder all night. She didn't want to bring it up in front of the kids.

"No." He folded his arms across his chest and leaned against the car. Amelia thought he could easily be one of those older, distinctive-looking models for fancy British leather shoes or some kind of spicy cologne. "We've got to interview the parents. That's never a good job."

"I'll bet." Amelia took a step closer to him. "Didn't they realize she had been missing since Friday?"

"How did you know that?" Dan asked, tilting his head to the right.

"Christine told me. How horrible those four days must have been for her parents." Amelia couldn't help but think of Adam and Meg. *How does a mother breathe when she knows her child is missing?* If she dwelled on the thought much longer, she was going to start crying.

"It's a funny thing. The parents didn't realize something was wrong until Sunday afternoon. Her boyfriend didn't call because he was out of town with his own job. That's already been verified. But Mr. and Mrs. Wilcox didn't know he was out of town. So, when Danielle didn't come home, they assumed she was with him. The two were serious enough. No engagement ring yet, but their relationship had all the telltale signs it was going in that direction. It was a missed one o'clock call, after twelve o'clock church services at St. Michael's Parish in Watsego, that Mr. and Mrs. Wilcox knew something was wrong."

"I don't understand." Amelia squinted.

"The Wilcoxes are devout Catholics," Dan explained. "But, since Danielle was young and out in the world, she didn't always go to mass at the same time or even at the same church as her parents. But they had a ritual that, no matter where she was, she'd call on Sunday after she got home from the latest church service. This time there was no call. Mrs. Wilcox immediately called the police."

"Is there any footage from surveillance or anything to help out?" Amelia quickly steered the conversation away from the emotions or the heart-break. Just the facts.

"No." Dan sighed. "Whoever did this did it quickly and either slipped out during the final minutes of business hours when everyone was leaving, just mingling in with the crowd, or the perp somehow managed to sneak out without being seen by surveillance at all."

"You've got your work cut out for you on this one." Amelia blinked.

"Tell me about it."

"If you'd like to stop by tomorrow you are more than welcome. Adam will be home, but Meg is spending the night with Katherine."

"On a school night?"

"Yeah. They are partners on some science project and begged and begged to put the final touches on it while having a sort of sleepover." Amelia smiled. "I'm sure by three o'clock they'll both be as grouchy as ever and ready for bed before the sun goes down."

"I'd love to. But it all depends on how things turn out with this case," Dan said.

Amelia noticed he was keeping pretty tightlipped about it. If he thought that she would throw caution to the wind just by hearing a few syllables of his opinions of the case, well, he wasn't totally wrong. Sure, she'd love to hear his take on the people at the MK factory. But she wasn't going to drag it out of him or drag her kids into it. That would be unhealthy for their relationship. Plus, she had Christine to talk to. There was more than one way to skin this cat.

"Can we play it by ear?" he asked.

"Sure. Thanks for dinner, Detective." She cupped Dan's cheek with affection then turned to head toward her front door.

"Wait just a minute." Dan held her hand firmly and pulled her toward him.

"No, no." She put her other hand over her mouth. "I had raw onions on my burger. I stink."

"So did I." Dan didn't loosen his grip.

"Yikes. Then it's you who stinks," Amelia teased.

Before she could make one final attempt to pull away, Dan slipped his arms around her waist and held her close to him. She looked up to his face, inhaling the scent of his skin and nervously fidgeting with his tie and lapel.

She had kissed Dan before. This was not a new development. But she couldn't help feeling the awkward butterflies in her stomach when he looked at her like he was now.

"Don't pull away, Ms. Harley," he purred. His eyes were gently stroking her face, and the left side of his mouth curled slightly. "Where do you think you're going?" As he leaned down, Amelia quit fighting and stood on tiptoes to meet him halfway in a passionate kiss goodnight.

"If I don't see you tomorrow, I'll call you."

Amelia nodded and reluctantly pulled her arms from around his neck—they had snuck up there, somehow. From the front door, she waved. Dan returned the gesture with a quick tap of his horn and drove off.

"Mom?" Meg was in the kitchen with one hand on her hip and the other holding her mother's cell phone. "It's Christine. She's been waiting for you for ten minutes."

"Ten minutes? I wasn't out there ten minutes."

"Ugh, you guys are so weird." Meg wrinkled her nose as she handed the phone to her mother then headed upstairs.

"Who's weird? Me and Dan or me and Christine?"

"Both!" Meg yelled from upstairs before her door clicked shut.

"Hey, girl." Amelia pulled a chair out from her kitchen table and took a seat. "How are you holding up?"

"Oh my gosh. Well, let me tell you, it's like a circus in the office. I don't mean to be... but there is work that still needs to get done," Christine complained. "Now that we are short-handed in the marketing department, everything is falling on me. I went to Lena to have her pull one of the girls from sales or accounting or something, just to help with the easy stuff, and my gosh. You'd think I was requesting they carry a Dixie cup of Ebola back and forth all day."

"People's brains probably haven't even totally wrapped around what happened." Amelia tried to sound supportive. "It will probably be like that for a couple of days."

"You're right." Christine gulped down something, probably wine. "My answer to a crisis or problem is to throw myself into some project. To me, it's like a waking nap. I'll focus on what has to get done, so my mind can get a break from focusing on the senseless murder that took place where I spend eight hours of my day, every day."

"So, since you spend all that time there, let me ask you a few things. Who is Lenny, and do you know him?"

"Lenny? Short guy, right?"

"Yeah, that's him." Amelia smoothed the back of her neck.

"I really don't talk to him. He's a bit of a jerk. I think he's in his early thirties, but he acts like a fourteen-year-old."

"He didn't seem too broken up about Danielle being killed."

"Ha, I'll bet he wasn't," Christine snapped. "Danielle didn't care for Lenny. He would leer at her, you know, when she walked past his cubicle. And he was always mentioning going out for a drink or meeting some people at a new place and she should come check it out. She used the word 'persistent.' I'd use the word pushy." Amelia could hear Christine's eyes roll. "Who in their right mind wants to dip their pen in company ink?"

"I couldn't agree more," Amelia concurred. John didn't meet Jennifer at work, but he did meet her when he was out to lunch—at work. "Did Danielle tell you about his invitations, or did you just hear it through the grapevine?"

"She told me herself." Christine cleared her throat. "At first, she kind of took it as a nice gesture. There are a number of assistants and a few of the warehouse guys who go down to Jack's on the corner on Fridays to toss back a few. The unofficial Christmas party is there every year, too, from what I hear."

"So why didn't she ever go?"

"Well, what she told me was that he invited her to go out to Jack's and told her a couple people from the office were going, too. But when Danielle started asking around, it turned out no one was going. It would just be her there. With Lenny. Alone. Like a date."

"Sneaky," Amelia crooned.

"Right? So, she decided she wasn't going to go. She told me she let Lenny know that no one was going and that she didn't feel comfortable going with him alone. Besides, she had a boyfriend. How would it look?"

"And what was his reply?"

"Typical for a jerk," Christine replied. "He made it up in his head that she was too much of a snob, she thought she was better than everyone else, yadda, yadda. But that didn't stop him from leering at her every time she walked by. I mean, she was a cute girl."

"Do you think he'd kill her for it?"

"I don't know. I talked to your friend, Detective Walishovsky. I told him about that, and he wrote it down, but I don't know what he thought of it."

"What do *you* think? In your gut," Amelia pushed, hoping to hear something that made sense and that might wrap this thing up sooner rather than later.

"My heart tells me that Lenny is really too much of a wimp to ever do that. You know the type from your dating days. All talk and no action," Christine joked. "But my head says sometimes a person just snaps."

Before Amelia could ask any more questions, she heard the sound of a mob of angry people bursting through the door at Christine's place.

"Okay! Do we need to shout as soon as we walk

in! I am on the phone!" Christine yelled. "Yes, hello. Hello. How was soccer? Who got in a fight? Well, who threw the mud first? Oh, well, those six-year-olds are vicious. Amelia, I gotta run. My house is being invaded by Pele and the gang."

"Sounds like fun." Amelia's words were smiling. "Tell the boys good job and love to Jason, too. I'll see you tomorrow at work."

"Absolutely."

Amelia sat at the kitchen table and mulled over what Christine had told her. Thinking back to her dating days was not all that thrilling, since as far back as she could remember, John had been the only real boyfriend she'd had.

But she could imagine what Lenny behaved like, just based on her observation of him today. She'd postpone judgment and sentencing until she had another chance to talk to the guy.

A damaged ego could fuel a fire of revenge quite easily. Danielle would not have thought anything of Lenny coming near her, since they did work together, and if she were like the majority of women when put in an awkward situation, she probably did the best she could to avoid eye contact, for fear it could spark a conversation. By then, it could have been too late for her to defend herself.

Amelia called to mind her own hurt feelings after her divorce. It frightened her a little to think that she had even considered violence. But there was something in her, the love for her children, the possibility of her own business, the upcoming season of *Better Call Saul*—these simple things kept her grounded. She might have imagined—and even enjoyed—the thought of causing physical harm to the man who dumped her so cruelly and the bimbo he dumped her for. However, the safety gauge was on.

In Danielle's case, Amelia was sure her assailant didn't have a safety gauge.

CHAPTER EIGHT

THE NEXT MORNING in front of the Master Ketchup factory, things were pretty much the same as they had been the day before. People trickled up to the food trucks to grab a breakfast or cupcake or much-needed coffees. They finished their cigarettes, got in their morning gossip, then headed inside once the factory whistle blew.

"I don't know if I'd like that kind of job," Lila offered as she washed the morning's mixing bowls. "Stopping and starting to the sound of a whistle reminds me too much of school."

"Really? You strike me as the kind of gal who would have liked school." Amelia took a drink of water.

"Ugh," Lila replied. "I hated school. There was

nothing they could teach me that I couldn't learn faster and better on the street."

"I'm not sure how to interpret that, Lila." Amelia looked at her suspiciously.

"Please, I wish I was that scandalous." Her shoulders bounced as she chuckled. "No. I mean I just don't like the confines of a cube."

"You'd hate this place. That's what they have in there. I saw them when I went peeking in there yesterday."

"Did you see anything else?"

"No. Heard a few things, but nothing I can really sink my teeth into."

Just then, loitering outside the factory, pacing back and forth between the alley and the Pink Cupcake's rear bumper, was the guy in the overalls who had sprinted across the street yesterday.

Amelia watched him as he strolled back and forth, looking at his watch and puffing a cigarette down to the filter. Finally, he saw what he'd been waiting for.

As everyone else was going into the building, the tight-skirted woman from yesterday emerged and began to walk across the street. Without nearly as much discretion as yesterday, they both headed off across the street.

Amelia watched.

"A little rendezvous before the nine o'clock conference call," Lila mused.

"Right? Did you see them go that way yesterday, too?"

Lila shook her head, but her right eyebrow, which she'd drawn on with care, arched deviously high and up to her forehead as she looked from Amelia to the couple.

Within minutes, the pair had come back into view. He jogged to the factory entrance off the alley, and she went through the front door. Amelia and Lila worked with no more noise than the bustle of the neighborhood around them.

Before she knew it, Amelia heard the midday whistle blowing.

"Can you handle the restless natives?" Amelia asked, pulling off her apron and stepping down the back steps of the truck.

"Of course. Where are you going?"

"Nowhere. But I'll be back in a minute."

Lila shrugged and went back to arranging the final batch of PB&J cupcakes next to the new Breakfast Dessert cupcakes, which had quickly become popular among the big-boned construction workers down the street.

Without wasting any time, Amelia ran down the same gangway she had seen the couple retreat down yesterday and this morning. It came to a dead end, unless a person wanted to scale the chain-link fence and risk the barbed wire at the top, or didn't mind giving their position away by yanking down the rusty fire escape ladder attached to the other building.

If Amelia didn't find a hiding place, she'd be seen by the shady couple.

"No," she mumbled as she stared at the large dumpster. The letters WM were painted in white on its dark-green body. Her heart was racing. Time was running out. *Just up and in. Climb that box, swing a leg over and, once you're inside, just crouch. Don't touch the sides. Simple.*

Looking over her shoulder, she saw people starting to emerge from all the buildings to take advantage of the weather and their fifteen-minute breaks.

Just do it!

Without thinking, Amelia stepped onto a red plastic milk crate, lifted the plastic lid of the dumpster, and swung one leg over before the smell hit her. Gasping a little, she took a gulp of air, swung her other leg over, and carefully pulled the lid down over her, just as the man in the overalls appeared at the street entrance.

There wasn't a ton of trash in the dumpster. Thankfully, most of it had been tossed to the side opposite Amelia. But as she crouched inside, she did start to feel herself sinking.

"What took you so long?" she heard the man say. Throwing caution to the wind, she put the very tips of her fingers against the lip of the dumpster and peeked out.

The woman was hurrying along. "I couldn't help it." She rushed up to him and, as Amelia predicted, kissed him full on the lips. "That detective called and said he wanted me to come down to the station."

"What? Why?" the man asked.

"I don't know. I think…" She hesitated. "Dean, I think they know."

"They would only know if you told them." Dean held her by her shoulders and looked in her eyes. "Did you tell them?"

"I don't think I did," she muttered.

"Well, what exactly did you say? You said something that's got them wanting to talk to you again. How come they aren't asking to talk to me?"

The woman shrugged. "If only Danielle would

have kept her mouth shut. Why did she have to stick her nose in our business?"

"So you told them Danielle knew about us? Is that it?" Dean asked. "Mindy? Is that what you said?"

"Well, if they found out and knew I lied, they might dig deeper. I didn't want them doing that. Right?" Mindy took a step closer to Dean. "I didn't want them to know that you've been in jail before." She reached up and ran her hand through Dean's sandy hair. "I mean, I helped get you this job. If they knew I put in a different background check, we'd both be in trouble. This way it keeps that safe."

Breathing through her mouth, Amelia listened to Dean and Mindy. It was only when she felt something cool and wet touch her ankle that she held her breath again.

"If they call me in to the police station, my wife is going to find out all about us," Dean whined. "She's going to know I was with you when I said I was with Kirk. The whole thing is going to blow up in our faces."

"Baby, no, it isn't." Mindy shook her head. "Baby, look at me. Neither one of us killed Danielle. They aren't looking for us."

"But our alibis are each other. My wife isn't going to understand if she finds out this way. We had a plan, remember? When my wife got back from having her shoulder surgery, I was going to tell her."

Amelia tried to control her gag reflex and stood stone still, making sure whatever was touching her ankle wasn't creeping up higher on its own. With every sense on high alert she felt something fall on her head. It didn't move. But there was definitely something stuck in her hair.

"Why do we have to wait?" Mindy whined. "Why don't we just go march down to the police station together? Holding hands. They'll see we are a united front and nothing can break us apart. Like Bon Jovi says, 'Never Say Goodbye.'"

Had Amelia not been partially distracted by what had fallen on her head and what was touching her ankle, she would have burst out laughing. This was daytime drama at its very best.

Before they could find any more lyrics to match their love, the break-time whistle blew. Amelia watched through the grimy slit between the lid and lip of the dumpster as Dean and Mindy quickly canoodled as though they were on the Titanic and it was getting ready to go down into the icy abyss.

Finally, they tore away from each other and, in a single file, headed back.

Amelia pulled herself out of the dumpster, brushed herself off, and slowly walked back to the Pink Cupcake.

"Did that girl beat you up?" Lila asked, squeezing lavender petals onto a fresh batch of vanilla-lavender cupcakes.

Amelia shook her head, reached into the emergency locker, and pulled a fresh hot-pink t-shirt from behind the first aid kit, an extra blanket, and couple of extra sets of oven mitts. "No." Amelia sighed and walked to the only private corner, behind the driver's seat. She pulled off her shirt and quickly slipped into the XL Pink Cupcake t-shirt of the same design that Lila was considering ordering in bulk for a special promotion around Christmas time. "I was hiding in the dumpster."

"You know, I really admire your hutzpah."

"Hutzpah? Where I come from, it's called stupidity." Amelia looked at her dirty shirt and stifled a gag. "Man, what is this? I tried not to touch anything. I didn't think I did, but I guess I was totally wrong. Totally." She wrinkled her nose and grimaced. "I'll bet I stink, too."

"I didn't want to say anything but, well... since you brought it up..."

"Oh, Lila, I'm sorry." She went to the sink and began to scrub her hands and arms, all the way up to her shoulders. She doused a clean wash rag with water and scoured her face, neck, and hair. "Thank goodness for this short haircut. I may not smell great, but this should at least make me bearable."

"No worries. I was with Rusty at the Twisted Spoke last night for their monthly Harley H.O.G. meeting. Believe me, some of those guys would do well to wash off in a sink once in a while." Lila pinched her nose while squeezing the frosting tube with the other. "Now, the real question is, what did you find out?"

Amelia stopped and looked at Lila, still holding the wet rag in her hand to drip, drip, drip on the floor. "You were with Rusty last night?"

"Please, get that *Peyton Place* look off your face. We became good friends after that whole *event* at his restaurant."

Amelia shrugged, giggling.

"I'm just glad you made a friend. That's all." Amelia told Lila about the dramatic exchange she overheard in the alley, complete with reenactments of their romantic gestures and, of course, "Never Say Goodbye."

"Okay, well, we know those two are probably too stupid to know anything more about the murder, not to mention being too stupid to know good music from bad." Lila shook her head. "Oh, how youth is wasted on the young."

CHAPTER NINE

"MOM, Christine called twice while you were in the shower," Adam said through the bathroom door.

"Okay, honey. Thanks," Amelia replied. She hoped neither of the kids would feel like a shower tonight, since she was sure she had used all the hot water in her efforts to completely scrub off the residue from the WM dumpster. She was pretty sure she had gotten every bug, germ and cootie off her skin. A healthy dose of honey-and-lavender lotion and a spritz of perfume made her feel like she'd just stepped out of a spa. Her terrycloth robe was a little worn, and a few stains from makeup and spilled sips of coffee graced the front, but Amelia just couldn't bear to part with it. Fuzzy slippers were the finishing touch.

She felt refreshed and rejuvenated, but what made her feel even better were the sounds from her kitchen.

"It's your turn, Adam," Meg instructed.

"Keep an eye on him, Meg," Dan replied. "I think he's going to choke on this one. He's definitely going to choke."

"Don't hate," Adam teased. "I've just got the skills is all."

"You mean skeeze," Meg replied.

"Hardy-har," Adam replied over the sound of dice toppling out of a cup. "Oh, yeah. Oh… wait."

Both Meg and Dan burst out laughing as whatever plan Adam had for squashing their chances at victory had itself been squashed.

"That is just wrong," Adam complained.

"I think you better just hand over the dice and let me show you how it's done," Dan instructed. His deep voice sounded funny when he was conversing with the kids. He never used words like *perpetrator*, *evidence*, *weapons*, or any other cop lingo around them. Dan made a special effort to let Meg and Adam just be themselves. They didn't have to grow up fast around him.

"What is going on down there? Are you guys giving my baby boy a hard time?"

"They are, Mom!" Adam yelled up the stairs.

"Adam's just a sore loser, Mom!" Meg added.

Amelia came down the stairs holding her robe tightly around her. As she came into his view, Dan looked at her as if she were wearing a ball gown and had spent four hours primping in the beauty salon.

"Dan brought Yahtzee over for us to play, and Adam stinks at this game," Meg offered happily.

"I'm afraid Meg is right," Dan added. "Adam does stink at this game."

"Well, you guys have ganged up on me. It's mental warfare, Mom."

"Now, you two, quit picking on my favorite son." Amelia pulled Adam to her by the shoulder and stroked his head hard, messing up his hair and making him laugh. "Otherwise, I'll have to bring down my other son that I've kept locked in the attic all these years."

"I think this game is just about over, anyway," Dan said as he collected the game pieces and the kids got up from the table.

"Thanks for the game, Dan," Meg said.

"Yeah, thanks, Dan," Adam added before skipping over to the basement door and heading down to his lair.

"Adam, can you show me that thing again?" Meg asked her big brother. They had been deep in conversation over the past few days about some computer game or app or something that Amelia had no idea about or interest in.

"Yeah. Come on." Adam and his sister went down into the darkness that was Adam's room.

"They'll be down there for a while." Amelia smiled. "Sorry for my appearance. I didn't think you'd make it by tonight."

"I think you look great," Dan said, standing up and walking over to Amelia to kiss her on top of the head.

"Would you like coffee?"

"Yes, ma'am."

Dan took a seat. After a few minutes of chatting, he brought up the Danielle Wilcox case. "I don't think you should keep showing up there," he said.

"What?" Amelia asked. "Why? What's happened?"

"Look, I can't get into all the details, but this case goes a little deeper than we first expected. The clues just aren't adding up the way they should be, and what we are learning, well, it just might not be the safest place."

"Are you telling the other food truck guys the same thing?" Amelia asked. "Are you really worried about everyone around, or is it just me? Because as much as I appreciate your concern, I don't see how I'd be in any more danger than the guys at Burger Rain or Damien's Hot Dogs."

"No." Dan sighed. "Amelia, I haven't said anything to the other truck drivers because I don't know them. I don't know their great kids or the way they look right after a really long shower. That probably isn't a great comparison, since the guys at those trucks weigh a combined total of two tons. But you know what I mean."

"I'm just there for Christine. It's just for this week, although the money is surprisingly good. I may make it part of my route."

"Promise me you'll be careful. Don't tell anyone about the kids or where you live. Don't wait around too long after everyone has left. Can you promise me that?"

"I can."

Amelia hated to admit it, but she was a little annoyed by Dan's pressure. Sure, he had made his feelings known before, but this was getting to be a little bit like John. *John? Do I really think that? Is Dan becoming possessive like John had been? Is it only a matter of time before Dan sees me as just an annoying thing in the way of what he wants to do?*

Amelia Harley, you stop being so hard on the guy, she thought to herself. *After what happened with Tim Casey, why in the world would you get mad at Dan for being concerned?*

"It's a little weird having someone looking out for me," she confessed.

"How do you think I feel?" Dan replied. "I'm not used to having someone to look out for. Well, I had a goldfish once."

"And what happened to him?"

"Leviathan? He got too big for his bowl, and I had to set him free in the ocean. He was eating me out of house and home."

Amelia laughed and asked Dan if he'd like to get in touch with his feminine side and help her with a new recipe she had been kicking around in her head. Before she could promise him first dibs on licking the bowl, Dan had slipped an apron over his head. "Tell me what to do."

That night, Amelia and Dan created the apple pie crumble cupcake.

"These are great," Christine mumbled through a mouthful as she stood outside the Pink Cupcake truck the next morning, attempting to pay.

"Your money's no good here, lady," Amelia said, waving away the five-dollar bill Christine tried to give her. "Hey, have you heard anything more about what's going on inside? Any new office gossip that might come in handy?"

Christine looked over her shoulder. As she did, both she and Amelia saw the cage-free-egg lady quickly approaching. Christine shook her head, pretended to be finished with her transaction, and meandered off to the side of the truck.

"Don't you have any more of the peanut butter and jelly cupcakes?" the woman asked, scanning over the list of daily specials. Her eyes narrowed as if she might have missed them.

"No. I'm sorry. But, please, have a sample of our new apple pie crumble cupcake. Everyone seems to like—"

"That isn't what I want. I want a peanut butter and jelly cupcake. Well, I guess you lose my business for today." She was about to walk away but turned on her heel and came back to the window. Amelia smiled, thinking maybe she was going to ask for the sample after all, but that wasn't it. "I've also reported your truck to the State of Oregon's Department of Agriculture and informed them you use caged eggs. You can expect a phone call."

Before Amelia even had time to let the words sink into her head, the woman had already stomped away in a huff.

"Did you hear that?" Amelia looked at Lila. "You did, right? I didn't just hallucinate that?"

"Oh my gosh." Christine came back up to the truck. "I can't believe she did that. She's such a pain."

Amelia huffed. "Who is that?"

"That's Joyce Ross. She's the secretarial manager. It's because of her I can't get any extra help." Christine rolled her eyes and took the last bite of her cupcake. "Her husband is one of the bigwigs on the third floor, so there is no getting around her. She's here for the duration. My boss, Lena, is terrified of her."

"What in the world is a secretarial manager?" Lila asked, staring daggers at the woman's back.

"She's in charge of the secretarial pool. I'm just glad I don't work as an assistant, because from the stories I've heard, she is a bit—how do I put it— drunk with power." Amelia offered Christine a napkin, which she took. She wiped her mouth. "Just about nine months ago they hired a girl to be an assistant to the assistants who help the CEO, CFO, Joyce's husband, all those guys. Well, this girl found out that Joyce's husband liked Harley-Davidson motorcycles. You'd have to be blind to not know it. He's got framed posters of them in his office." Christine rolled her eyes. "Anyway, this girl had a book on motorcycles she didn't want anymore, so she gave it to him, just in a nice gesture. No harm or malice intended. Joyce had her fired the very next day."

"Are you sure that was the reason?" Amelia squinted. "Maybe the girl wasn't any good or talked back or something."

"No, I'm sure, because I had to give Payroll a detailed list of everything the girl had done for the marketing department for the pay period. That kind of sneakiness only happens when management doesn't really have a reason to let someone go. They comb through every hour you've worked and say, 'Oh, look, on Tuesday June 8th, you didn't send a fax and that cost us eight million dollars, so you're fired.'"

Amelia shook her head.

"I am so glad I don't work in an office," Lila said.

"That makes two of us. Was Danielle working at the time this girl was fired?" Amelia folded her arms over her chest. "If Danielle was there and had any input or anything on this other secretary who helped her get fired, maybe revenge on Danielle was the motive."

"I can't remember for sure. But it shouldn't be too hard to find out."

"Do you know if Mr. Ross *has* had any flings with any of the women here?" Amelia shook her head. "It's such a cliché, but it happens all the time."

"As far as I know, the guy has never done anything. They drive in and park in the garage where all the bosses park their cars. They are always together, except when they're working. But then again, what do I know? I am here to work. I try to keep my nose out of it all, because it's never as cut and dried as you think it is."

"Right," Amelia mused. "Do you think you could get me the name of the girl who was fired, and maybe an address? It wouldn't hurt to talk to her."

"Sure." Christine looked at her watch. "I gotta run. I won't see you at break time, because I'm working through in order to leave early. The kids have some school play I have to go to."

"Don't you enjoy seeing those?" Amelia joked. "I always liked watching Adam's cheeks flush red when he had to speak a line or Meg gush with dramatic pauses that would make William Shatner jealous."

"Yeah, well, my kids like to ad-lib. A lot. And not all of it is appropriate for young viewers." Christine rolled her eyes and tried not to chuckle. She waved goodbye and left Amelia and Lila alone.

"So, I think I'll wait for the name of that girl who got fired and check out that angle." Amelia looked at Lila, who was searching for something on her phone. "What are you looking for?"

"I have a farmer friend who owns a lavender field. I just want to check out this whole Department of Agriculture business. He'll know who to talk to. But I think it is a safe bet to call B.S. on that Joyce woman's allegation."

"I hope you're right." Amelia clicked her tongue in annoyance. "I followed every step in order to get my license, and some nonsense like that shouldn't be a factor. City Hall would have told me, right? And they aren't caged eggs, for heaven's sake. They'd be caged chickens. Not eggs."

CHAPTER TEN

RAIN POURED down in thick sheets, pounding the sidewalk and giving the buildings a thorough wash.

"Gosh, I didn't even know it was supposed to rain." Amelia shook her head. "I haven't watched television or checked the news in days. For all I know, we've been at war and I wouldn't even know it."

"We live in Oregon. No need to check the weather. There is always a fifty-fifty chance of rain," Lila joked.

Just then, Amelia's phone rang. She smiled when she saw the name.

"I can tell that's not John calling," Lila teased, busying herself by taking inventory of their supplies. "We're running dangerously low on sugar."

Amelia nodded as she answered. "Hello?"

"It looks like the game is called off on account of rain," Dan said in his usual, no-nonsense tone of voice.

"Yeah, it looks that way. I think we will probably end up closing shop early. Lila just told me we're almost out of sugar, so it wouldn't be a bad idea."

"That sounds perfect."

"Perfect?" Amelia screwed up her face. "Crazy as it may seem, I don't get paid for my good looks. I think I need to invest in an awning to attach to the truck. What do you think?"

"I think we should talk about it over lunch."

"Okay." Amelia pulled the phone from her ear and held it to her chest. "You can go on home early today, Lila. Can I bother you to pick up some sugar on the way?"

"As soon as I wrap up the books, I'll be happy to. I'll take the receipts with me and balance everything when I get home. Sound okay?"

"You're an angel from heaven." Amelia put the phone back to her ear. "I'll meet you at Moody's?"

"See, it's that kind of mind reading that makes me nervous around you," Dan said.

"Well, a man should never be too comfortable around his woman. It breeds complacency," Amelia replied.

Dan chuckled and hung up the phone.

Moody's was across town but worth battling the traffic and red lights for. They had the most amazing Italian subs, which Amelia almost loved as much as her own flesh-and-blood children. When she pulled the big truck up to the curb and put it in park, Dan came strutting out of the restaurant with an umbrella.

"Can you believe this weather?" He grinned.

"Well, you look mighty happy to be in a rainstorm." Amelia ducked her head and slipped her arm through Dan's, snuggling close to him as they both shuffled quickly into the restaurant. It was a rustic place with a blazing fireplace in the middle of the dining area.

"Your table's ready, Detective." The waitress smiled. "Hi, Amelia."

"Thanks." Dan took Amelia's hand as they walked to a quiet table for two in a dark corner of the restaurant.

After they ordered their food, Amelia leaned in toward the detective. "So, I'm not sure if I should be nervous or happy about that grin on your face. Are you going to tell me the good news or what?"

"We made an arrest in the murder of Danielle Wilcox."

"What? When? Who?"

"His name is Charles Howe."

"Christine never mentioned him. Who is he? What happened?" Amelia leaned into the table even further.

"Charles had quite a crush on Danielle," Dan replied. "According to several sources, he was a bit of a screw-up before she started working there... Showing up late. A bit of backtalk to the supervisors in the mailroom. Breaking dress-code. Nothing that was enough to get him fired, but it was enough to make people notice when all his shenanigans stopped after Danielle started working there. He got a shave and a haircut. Began coming in early and not leaving until Danielle did, and that was sometimes five or ten minutes after everyone else. His latest review boasted as perfect a score as any employee at a place like this could get. Everyone noticed the change. Danielle noticed the change."

"She didn't like him? I had heard she had a boyfriend, but sometimes girls just say that so they don't hurt a guy's feelings."

"I'm afraid she liked the attention, but it didn't do her any good. They were seen together at several gatherings after work, sitting together and talking intimately. Sort of like you and I are right now." Dan winked at her. "A few people said they saw them leave places together, but no one could confirm they were an item."

"But if he liked her and went through all these positive changes, why would he kill her? What pushed him over the edge?" Amelia asked through a mouthful of sandwich.

"When we went to Charles's apartment, we found over two dozen pictures of Danielle tacked up on his wall. Some of them she posed for at work with other people. But most of them were taken when she was unaware. Some were innocent enough, of her sitting at her desk or eating lunch. Some were a little more scandalous, where she was bending over or stretching up to reach something in the supply room. The date on the picture of her on the stepladder in the supply room was the day Danielle was murdered."

Amelia gasped and began to cough as part of her sandwich went down the wrong pipe. She finally got the words out. "What a stroke of luck! So he was the last one to see her. What do you think happened?"

"I think Charles had it in his head that he wasn't going to take no for an answer this time. I think he approached her, asked her out for what was probably the hundredth time, and she said no, again, for the hundredth time. It didn't sit well with him. He probably started to argue with her, and before either of them knew what happened, he'd grabbed the box cutter, took a swipe, and slit her throat. Everyone was gone from the building already. He just shut the door to the supply room, as if nothing had happened, and walked out." Dan took a bite of his sandwich and a sip of his pop from a big red plastic cup.

Before Amelia could ask another question, her phone began to ring. It was her ex-husband, John. "Excuse me, Dan. It's the kids' father."

Dan nodded and dug into his food as he watched Amelia's face.

"Hi, John," Amelia snapped quickly. "What kind of problem?"

Dan stopped chewing and swallowed hard. He leaned back in his seat.

"Well, you need to tell her that you aren't going to do that. John, Adam has already written a speech. He's got a date he's bringing. Oh, my… you can't be serious?" Amelia looked at Dan with tears in her eyes. "I can't even begin to count all the times you told *us* no, and you won't tell Jennifer no to this one thing? Are you absolutely kidding me?"

Squaring her shoulders, Amelia lifted her chin but looked into space, not wanting to see Dan for fear she'd lose her composure. "John, he is your oldest and only son. If past behavior dictates anything, you'll have another wife in short order. But you will not have another Adam. If you don't make this right, you'll… What do you mean, 'don't take this tone' with you? It's high time I did. I'm warning you, John. Do not do this to Adam."

Amelia bit her tongue to keep the tears back behind her eyes. She didn't want to break down in front of Dan. She had never done that. Her relationship with her ex-husband was just a small avenue she had to go down every once in a while, and usually there was no need to involve Dan in it. But she wasn't sure how she'd be able to keep this from him, since the whole horrible story was probably written all over her face.

"I'm not saying a word to him. This your decision. You have to tell him, if you are going to go through with it. But I'm begging you, John. Don't break your son's heart like this. Don't do it."

It was obvious from her reaction that John had hung up on Amelia. She took the napkin from her lap and dabbed her eyes. "Jennifer told John she wanted her brother to be his best man, not Adam." Her bottom lip began to quiver. "How could he even entertain the idea, Dan? How could he turn his own son away?" She began to cry. "I'm sorry. I was having such a nice time with you. If only I hadn't answered my phone." She slapped her forehead with her hand.

"Well, it probably isn't my place, Amelia," Dan almost whispered, "because I'm an outsider. We've known each other for a while, but as for a real history together, well, that is still being made. But I know one thing. If Adam were my son, there wouldn't be a day that went by I didn't feel proud of that blessing." Dan's eyes teared as he spoke, and Amelia could see his underlying anger at John roll in like the thunderclouds that darkened the sky earlier today.

Amelia took his hand and kissed it. "You are a gem, Detective Walishovsky." She dabbed her eyes and began to clean up the table in front of her. "I don't know what I'm going to do."

"Do what you said. If John wants to make this mistake, it is his to make. It's not your job to make it easy on him. Maybe he just needed to hear it from you. I'll bet he has a change of heart and Adam will be his best man at the wedding. You might get the blame for it, but that's a small price to pay."

Amelia nodded and sniffed. Dan was probably right. This would blow over, and the wedding would go off like the conversation never took place.

That afternoon, after kissing Dan goodbye on the porch as the rain continued in a light drizzle but with even darker clouds rolling in, she called Christine.

"What do you mean, they arrested Charles?" Christine asked. "Charles couldn't have done it. I don't believe it."

"They said that he had a picture of Danielle standing on a ladder in the supply room on the day of the murder. You have to admit that that is pretty coincidental. He was the last person to see her alive."

"I don't care if he had the box cutter in his pocket. I don't believe it," Christine insisted. "Charles and Danielle were friends."

"The police seem to think that Charles wanted to be more than friends with her. You know how that story goes? He's into her, but she's not into him. It gets out of hand when he gets rejected that last time, and next thing you know, someone's throat is slit." Amelia poured herself half a glass of wine. "Happens all the time. Just watch the true crime channel and you'll see."

"Yes, in other places. But not this time. Not Charles and Danielle," Christine said. "From what I heard about those two, it was like they were brother and sister. Just two people who found each other and were smart enough to know they were better friends than anything else. They didn't sneak around. They didn't keep their friendship quiet. Everyone knew they were pals."

"But what about Dan saying Charles had pictures of Danielle all over his apartment? What do you think of that?" Amelia sipped her wine.

"Look, I'm an inch away from killing my own children every day, but I've got their pictures all over my house. Now, if Charles had pictures of Danielle with her eyes scratched out or scribbles over images, then I might wonder. But were these framed? Were they on a dartboard, or the fridge? I mean, Charles came out of his shell when Danielle started working at Master Ketchup. I don't know what that means, but he didn't act like a guy who only had eyes for her. He acted like a guy who was told by a pretty girl that he could easily find another pretty girl, and he believed her. They were like cheerleaders for each other."

"Kind of like you and me," Amelia said.

"Exactly." Christine's voice smiled. "That's why I say they were like brother and sister. Like Meg and Adam would be if they worked together."

That was all it took. Suddenly the murder, the arrest of Charles Howe, the whole mess melted away as Amelia's eyes blurred with tears and she began to sob.

"My gosh! Amelia! What did I say?" Christine blubbered. "What's the matter?"

"Oh, Christine, you aren't going to believe this." She clenched her teeth and tried to push her emotions back just long enough to tell Christine about the phone call she had with John.

"That witch," Christine spat.

"I don't completely blame her, Chris. She wouldn't even have had the gall to ask such a thing if John hadn't made it clear it was okay to do. What is wrong with him? These are his children!"

Christine clicked her tongue. "Maybe it's just talk. Maybe the little twerp is just so overwhelmed with the wedding plans that she's talking out of the hole in her head and John just wants to let it blow over, you know? Let her come to her senses on her own. Maybe she will. It's a long shot, I know, but maybe?"

"Oh, I hope so, Christine, because if it isn't, I just don't even want to think of how Adam is going to feel. He already wrote a speech, and he read it to me. It's beautiful, with memories and stories about things that went on between the two of them, and you'd have to have a heart of stone not to hear the love in it." Amelia sniffed. "Love that two-timer doesn't deserve."

Just as Amelia was about to go on an obscenities-filled tirade about her ex-husband, the front door opened and slammed shut. Then it opened again. "Thanks, jerk!" Meg yelled at her brother, who stomped into the house ahead of her, making a beeline for his room in the basement. His eyes were red, and he didn't look at Amelia when she called to him. He just slammed his door shut and pounded down the stairs.

Amelia looked at Meg.

"Don't ask me." She shrugged. "He didn't say anything to me or Amy the whole ride home on the bus. I didn't do anything to him, so I don't know why he's slamming the door shut on me."

"Oh, Christine." Amelia gritted her teeth. "I think John called Adam at school."

Her blood raced, and she felt like getting in her car, driving to Jennifer's house, dragging her out into the yard by her hair, and slapping her senseless while daring John to stop her.

"What a class act." Christine hissed. "Look, let me give you the address of that employee who got fired. You still want it, right?"

"Yeah," Amelia mumbled distractedly. "Give the details to Meg for me. I'm going to check on Adam." Amelia handed the phone to her daughter, who cheerfully chirped a hello to her Auntie Christine and took down all the information Christine gave her.

Meg then proceeded to tell Christine how her best friend Katherine had to be rushed to the hospital to have a splinter, which she had gotten while hiking almost three weeks ago, removed after it had become infected. "No, they didn't have to amputate," Meg said, but apparently it was in a kind of embarrassing place. "Yes, her butt."

CHAPTER ELEVEN

THE LAMP on Adam's nightstand was on, in addition to his three computer screens. He sat in his chair in front of them, quickly tapping away as if he were trying to stop the computer at NORAD from launching nuclear missiles at Russia.

"Adam." Amelia took a seat on his bed behind him. "What's the matter?"

He didn't answer.

"I spoke with your dad today." She watched as his hands stopped typing. He put them in his lap, and his shoulders slumped. He reached into his pocket, took out his cell phone and handed it to his mother.

She looked at it and saw there was one saved message.

Really, John! You left it on his voicemail! Reluctantly she hit the button to hear the message and nearly screamed with frustration when she heard John's voice, which said, "I just need you to be an adult about this, Adam. Jennifer wants you to handle the guestbook. That is a huge honor in her family. So, you can still wear the tuxedo and—"

Amelia pulled the phone away from her ear. "Adam, your dad is…"

"I know what you're going to say, Mom." He sniffed.

"No, I don't think you do." She swallowed hard. "Your dad is making some very bad decisions right now. I'm going to leave this to you to handle. Whatever you decide you want to do is one hundred percent fine with me. You're almost old enough to join the service and die for your country. You can certainly decide how you'd like to handle this wedding and your relationship with your father. Whatever you decide, I'll support you… as long as it doesn't require that I consult a lawyer."

"Mom?" Adam turned and looked at his mother.

Normally, she saw the handsome face of her ex-husband when she looked at her son. But this time she saw the little boy she fell in love with the first time she felt him kick in her belly. He was hurt and vulnerable, and there was nothing she could do to help. At least she didn't think so. "Yes, honey?"

"I'll go to the wedding and do this. But can you pick me up after the ceremony? I don't want to go to the reception."

"Well, I think that's a very mature response. Absolutely. And if you change your mind, that's okay, too. Whatever you want."

Adam nodded and turned back to his screen, wiping his eyes and focusing on the screens in front of him. Amelia pushed herself off the bed, kissed Adam on the head, and walked over to the stairs.

"Mom?"

"Yes?"

"Dad made a bad decision when he left us."

Amelia wanted to run to her son and scoop him up in her arms, squeeze him tightly and smother him with kisses. Instead, she choked her tears back and smiled. "I couldn't agree more."

As she opened the door to the basement and stepped into the family room, Amelia found Meg sitting on the edge of the couch with a worried expression on her face.

"Did you hear any of that?" Amelia asked, smoothing her daughter's hair back from her ears.

"I heard part of it. What did Dad do?"

Amelia explained the situation to her daughter with as much tact and compassion toward John and Jennifer as she could muster without making herself throw up. She did clear her throat twice in order to suppress her gag reflex.

"I don't want to stay for the reception if Adam isn't going to." Meg pushed her shoulders back as she spoke. "We're a team."

Unlike her daughter, who was not emotional but pillar-strong, Amelia felt a new flood of warm tears surface in her own eyes. "I'll tell you what I told Adam. Whatever you and your brother decide, I'll support it. No matter what." Amelia smiled and wiped a tear from her cheek.

"That's because we're a team, Mom. All of us." Meg hopped up and kissed her mom on the cheek before handing her a Post-it note, strutting confidently out of the room, then pounding up the steps to her own room.

Amelia looked down and read the name *Vivika Korseky* with an address in New Lenox, the next town over. Meg dotted the "i's" with hearts. There was a phone number, too.

Normally, Amelia would hop in her car, head on over to this woman's house, and invite herself in for a little chat. But with all the aggravation over the past couple of hours, due to John and his pitiful behavior toward his children, she was exhausted, so instead, she picked up the phone and dialed the number.

"Hello." Amelia cleared her throat. She thought her own voice sounded like she had gone forty-eight hours with no sleep. That certainly was how she felt. "This message is for Vivika Korseky." She introduced herself. "I'm wondering if you could meet with me for a few minutes to talk about Master Ketchup." Before she left her phone number, Amelia did mention the murder.

When she hung up the phone she walked to the fridge, looked inside the freezer, and pulled out some frozen beef stew she had made a week earlier, along with a loaf of Italian bread.

"Comfort food. I think that's what we all need."

———————————

At work the following morning, Lila shouted loudly enough for everyone within six miles to hear. "He did what?!" She stared at Amelia. "To his own son? Well, I knew John could be difficult, but I thought when it came to the kids that he drew the line."

"Believe me, so did I." Amelia scooped the batter for a batch of apple pie crumbles into the hot-pink, ruffled paper cups that sat daintily in the muffin tin.

"You know what, Amelia?" Lila said as she slowly mixed the cinnamon, dried apples, vanilla extract, sugar, egg and flour together for the crumbly top part of the cupcakes. "This may be the beginning of the end, if you know what I mean."

"Yes. I do." Amelia pouted. "I think the kids do, too. But I'm the one left holding the bag. I'm the one who has to tell them that... that their father has moved on. Lila, he was doing so well. *We* were doing so well. I mean, he was there for the kids every weekend, they did fun family things, we spoke to each other civilly. What in the world kind of bee got in his bonnet?"

"The tan, twenty-five-year-old kind." Lila clicked her tongue in disgust.

"I'm telling you, Lila, I was so mad last night that I couldn't even think straight. I was contemplating going to John's house. I was ready to make the biggest scene in the history of ex-wives making big scenes. Cops would be involved, and I can't promise I wouldn't have called you to post my bail."

"You know I would," Lila replied with as much

seriousness in her voice as if she were taking an oath with her hand on the Good Book.

"But then what would the kids do? I can't do anything. I can't fix this. I can't make their hearts not hurt. All I can do is be there to pick up the pieces. What the heck, Lila?"

"Look. You've done some amazing things since I've known you. This business is keeping us both in a pleasant financial place. You've met a man who really seems to appreciate everything about you, and that includes those beautiful kids of yours who, when I see them, are laughing, talking, smiling. That is the real success, Amelia. Those kids are happy when they are with you."

"But children deserve a mother and a father." Amelia pulled out one batch of double-fudge cupcakes and grabbed the raspberry glaze. "It's what all the television talk shows say. Even a bad father is better than none."

"They need a father figure, Amelia, and they have one. A man who really wants to be with them." Lila winked.

Even though she didn't say Dan's name, Amelia nearly burst out crying. She hugged her friend tightly and kissed her on the cheek. "Lila, you are worth your weight in gold."

"Funny, Rusty told me that yesterday while we were enjoying a couple of beers together."

"How are things going with you two?" Amelia felt better and no longer wanted to talk about herself. She was much more interested in her employee's personal business.

"We actually have a lot in common."

Aside from the red hair—Lila's was dyed, and Rusty's was almost all gray—Amelia couldn't imagine an odder couple. But yet they did somehow look like they belonged together. Maybe not in a romantic way, as Lila seemed to insinuate. They were just two people who knew how to talk and carry on a good conversation.

As Lila went on about possibly taking a bike trip with Rusty to Sturgis in South Dakota next year, Amelia laid out the cupcakes for the quickly approaching factory employees. Ten o'clock on the dot was break time.

Christine approached the truck as usual and snuck around to the side entrance. "What's going on, gals?"

"We're plotting John's unsolved disappearance. Care to join us?" Lila joked, making Amelia laugh and shake her head.

"I'll take a piece of that action," Christine concurred.

Amelia turned to her and offered her a warm chocolate-raspberry cupcake, hot out of the oven.

"Amelia, I'm going to get so fat if you don't find another corner to work on soon."

Lila shuffled from one foot to the other as she counted out some change to a young man from the factory across the street who'd bought three cupcakes.

"What's wrong with you?" Amelia asked.

"Too much coffee this morning. I need to get to the bathroom, but I can't imagine using those porta-johns."

"My gosh, no, Lila. Come with me." Christine offered her hand to the older woman. "Use the one in the factory. Come on. I'll take you there."

Amelia smiled as her oldest best friend and her newest best friend shuffled off down the sidewalk and into the building like a modern-day Lucy and Ethel. The thought made her laugh until an odd scene caught her attention.

It was that mousy woman from the other day who'd acted like Oliver asking for more gruel at the orphanage when she bought three cupcakes. She was standing at the lip of the alley, watching everyone as they smoked their cigarettes or ate their cupcakes and chatted. No one engaged her. No one except Amelia seemed to even notice she was there.

Her solitude didn't seem to be a burden to her, either. Amelia watched as she began to mumble to herself, shrugging and shaking her head. There was a pretty intense conversation taking place, but only one participant. This wasn't normal behavior. This was a person who was nervous about something.

While she worked, she continued to watch the woman, who poked a thin white finger against the brick wall and traced the grooves of cement between each brick.

Before Amelia could approach her, Christine and Lila came hurrying back.

"Charles was put on suicide watch!" Christine exclaimed. "I just saw it on the receptionist's phone. They said he tried to kill himself last night."

"That's just horrible," Amelia said, her eyes still on the twitchy broad at the alley entrance.

"I'm telling you, as sure as I'm standing here, he didn't do it," Christine barked.

"I don't know," Lila said. "I certainly don't know the guy, but an attempted suicide doesn't usually look good."

"No, it doesn't," Christine admitted. "But I still can't believe it."

"Hey, Christine," Amelia interrupted, "who is that woman?" She discreetly pointed toward the alley.

"Oh, her. That's Penny Delmar," Christine said, squinting her eyes. "She has been promoted due to Danielle's, you know, no longer being with us."

"That's one heck of a way to get a promotion." Lila snickered.

Christine took a seat on the metal stool at the very back of the truck.

"Really? Is she a good secretary?" Amelia asked. *Would a promotion be enough of a reason to kill someone? Especially a secretarial promotion? Weird, but people have killed for less.*

"I don't know." Christine looked at her watch. "Joyce keeps the secretarial pool at drought levels for the marketing department. I gotta run. Back to the salt mines." She blew kisses and hurried off down the sidewalk and back into the building, as did the rest of the people, including pitiful Penny, who brought up the rear.

CHAPTER TWELVE

THAT EVENING, the rain had returned, but not in such force as the day before. It was enough to make everyone walk a little faster. Umbrellas and ponchos were at the ready, but most of the raindrops could be outrun.

Lila had finished the receipts and left with a hint that she was meeting Rusty for a burger at the Twisted Spoke.

Amelia cleaned up to get the truck ready for the morning rush. She was contemplating what to make and was afraid that some of her creations were getting too routine. The PB&J cupcake was a blockbuster, but she wanted something new. The chocolate and bacon was a hit, too. The apple pie crumble cupcake was like a slice of Americana, but it too was a familiar taste. She was never satisfied, always striving for the next flavor. What could she come up with that was like a step back into childhood, but with a grown-up flair?

Her mind replayed some of her favorite treats as a kid and some that remained guilty pleasures as an adult. Butterscotch pudding. Caramel Cow Tales. Oreo cookies. Bubblegum. Spaghetti with meatballs.

As she daydreamed, she watched the people from Master Ketchup file out of the building. Another day's work done. Some jumped into waiting cars, and others climbed into their own vehicles. Some headed off to the bus stop or to the train station a couple blocks down, and others walked to less-specific destinations.

That was the case with Penny Delmar. She straggled out of the revolving door like a baby bird that had landed with a thud before figuring out how to spread its wings. She didn't get in a car or head toward the train or bus stop. Instead, she looked around nervously and headed in the opposite direction from everyone else.

Amelia watched her and thought to follow her. With the skill and precision of someone who knew exactly what she was doing, Amelia quickly closed up the Pink Cupcake, locking the service window, the back door, the driver and passenger doors, still with enough time before Penny was out of sight to polish the side mirrors and wipe down the chalk-board menu to a clean black slate ready for what-ever they would serve up tomorrow.

With her purse over her shoulder, Amelia jaywalked across the street and watched from a hundred paces as Penny headed toward her destina-tion. From what Amelia could see, the girl was having a very heated discussion. Her hands were waving, and her head was tilting from side to side. *Is she deranged? Does she have a mental problem? Is she dangerous?*

Amelia wasn't sure, but as a precaution she slipped her hand into her purse. Within a second she found her pepper spray and held it tightly inside her palm. The neighborhood was a little iffy when the factories were shutting down, anyway. Penny looked like she might be stronger than what she looked like at first glance.

For two long city blocks, Amelia followed Penny deeper into the industrial neighborhood. But after another three blocks, small brick bungalow homes started popping up. Yards with statues of the Blessed Virgin, flowerpots, red, white and green flags hanging beneath Old Glory, and overgrown tomato plants were the norm. There were corner grocers that advertised sales on Genoa salami and capicola, fresh calamari, homemade cannoli and tiramisu, plus t-shirts that read "Proud to be Italian" and "Italian Princess" in the same red, white and green colors as the flags hanging from porches.

Penny picked up her pace, making Amelia wonder if she lived around here. But when Penny turned to the left and disappeared, Amelia saw she didn't go into a house or a store. She had almost broken into a run to get inside Saint Rocco's Catholic Church.

Amelia climbed the short steps to the heavy wooden double doors, took hold of one of the thick metal handles, and pulled. The door swung open easily. Her eyes adjusted to the dark atmosphere as her hand instinctively felt for the small cup of holy water that flanked the doors to the chapel.

It was a soothing place, with the glow of candles and the smell of incense engulfing Amelia completely. There were a few people scattered throughout the pews. Some were kneeling. Some were sitting. All had the rosary beads in their hands as they recited their prayers, looking up at the image of Jesus at the front of the church.

Penny was sitting at the very end of the last pew, closest to the statue of St. Michael the Archangel. It was as though she had folded herself up and had become thinner and smaller than she was as she shuffled down the street. She was crying.

Amelia quietly walked up to the pew, genuflected as was custom, and crossed herself before she stepped in and scooted over to Penny's side.

With wide, scared bug eyes, Penny stared at Amelia for a second. "What? Why are you following me?" Penny sniffled as quietly as possible, but her voice betrayed her, letting the anger show. She ruffled like an agitated hen.

"I'm sorry," Amelia whispered. "My name is Amelia Harley."

"You're from that pink food truck. What are you bothering me for? Don't you have some cupcakes to sell or something?"

Amelia couldn't hide her surprise. She would have never pegged Penny to be so smart-alecky.

"I saw you today, and you looked… Well, you looked very upset. I thought I might be able to help." It sounded lame, but it was the truth.

"Can you go back in time? Because that's the only thing that will help." Penny used the back of her hand to wipe her nose.

"No," Amelia said sadly, sticking her pepper spray back in her purse and pulling out a tissue instead. She handed it to Penny. "Sorry, but I can't do that. No one can. Why do you want to go back in time?"

Penny took the tissue and crumpled it in her hand. "Because then maybe Danielle wouldn't be dead." She sniffed as more tears rolled down her cheeks.

"You mean Danielle Wilcox? At work. Why would you say that?" Amelia scooted closer to Penny.

"It's my fault. She'd still be alive if it weren't for me." Penny's voice was barely above a whisper. It was obvious she had been holding this in since the news of Danielle's murder came out.

"What do you mean?" Amelia spoke softly, as if she were talking to Meg at five years old.

"I called in sick that day," Penny whispered. "I called in sick on Friday, even though I wasn't really sick. I wanted to go to the movies with my boyfriend. He works nights as an orderly at St. Joe's Hospital. I called in sick so I could be with him." She swallowed as if she were waiting for the accusations to start piling on.

"So, you weren't at work on Friday? That's...

okay. You didn't have anything to do with what happened."

"But I did," she mumbled. Her eyes rippled when she looked up at Amelia. Her bottom lip trembled madly, and the tip of her nose was bright red from crying. "If I had shown up, it would have been me putting the late delivery away. That was my job. Danielle was only in the supply room because she was doing what I should have been doing. It's because I lied. It's no different than if I had done the killing."

"Oh, honey, no." Amelia slipped her arm around Penny.

For a moment, she went rigid, as if the touch from another person might give her cooties or cause her skin to turn black. But after a moment, she relaxed. Then she sighed. Then she began to weep again. "It was supposed to be me." Penny's voice hitched in her throat.

"No. That isn't true. It wasn't supposed to be you." Amelia didn't have to raise her voice. The slightest sound echoed throughout the church.

"They gave me Danielle's job." Penny tried to keep it together. Her body was starting to tremble, and her eyes no longer saw Amelia but stared ahead of her as if she were watching some scary movie.

"What?" Amelia was shocked. This didn't sound right.

"Joyce told me I was being promoted." She shook her head. "I don't know what to do. I can't sit at Danielle's desk or use her computer. It feels funny, like I stole it. The files are all in her handwriting. The notes and instructions have her signature. They left her *nameplate* on the desk. I'm afraid to get rid of it. I can't just throw it away, right? What kind of person does that?" She leaned into Amelia and cried miserably.

Amelia didn't understand how the human resources department at Master Ketchup could be so unprofessional. It was obvious that Penny was going through some kind of post-traumatic stress disorder due to this murder. She was cracking up. To be told that she had to take the dead woman's place without a mourning period, without some kind of slow transition, was ludicrous.

"Penny, my friend Christine Mills works in the marketing department. Would you mind if I told her I spoke with you and asked her to help?"

"What can she do?"

"Honey, I think you are in shock over this murder. No one can blame you for it. It is a completely normal response, especially when you feel that you might somehow be at fault." Amelia took Penny's hands in hers. "First, your calling in sick had nothing to do with it. Believe me. We all need a mental holiday once in a while. But I don't think the folks at Master Ketchup thought this through. You're being asked to deal with something overwhelming. Christine will help you find the right person to talk to. I wouldn't know who that is. Is that okay?"

Penny's eyes lightened when she looked up at Amelia. "Do you think they'll fire me?"

"Not unless they want a lawsuit," Amelia barked before thinking, causing a few of the parishioners to look in her direction. "No. I'll bet Human Resources just made a mistake."

"It wasn't Human Resources who sent me to Danielle's desk."

"Isn't that who handles all the paperwork for promotions and raises and department numbers and stuff?"

"Yes. But I answer to Joyce Ross. She just assigned me to Danielle's job and walked away. Believe me, I was very happy where I was in the accounting department."

Amelia recalled her brief experiences with Joyce Ross and thought the woman probably didn't think things through. Perhaps she was in a state of shock, as well. Either way, Amelia was sure that Penny had nothing to do with Danielle's death. "Okay. Well, Christine can still help, and she'll be discreet. I've known her half my life, and believe me when I tell you if I ask her to keep a secret, she will."

"Thank you, Amelia. I think your advice is as good as your cupcakes. Those are all delicious, by the way."

Amelia thanked Penny, reassured her that everything was going to be fine, and left her in the church to finish her prayers.

Outside, Amelia saw a beautiful fiery sunset in the west that blew up the sky with rich pinks, oranges and purples as the sun reflected off the clouds that had covered the sky all day. She whispered a little prayer of thanks herself and quickly made her way back to the Pink Cupcake. As she drove home, she dialed Christine's number and gave her Penny's story.

CHAPTER THIRTEEN

THE NEXT DAY seemed calm in front of Master Ketchup. Amelia had yet to come up with a new recipe, but off-the-wall combinations like lime and cinnamon or cherry and maple kept coming. They weren't right. She was like a writer with writer's block, and it was driving her batty. Sales were still excellent, and it tickled Amelia as she watched Lila tell the construction workers from down the street that tomorrow would be their last day at this location.

"Well, I only come here to see your pretty face," one beer-bellied fellow with two chins and twinkling eyes replied. "What am I supposed to do now?"

Another fellow asked her if she'd teach him how

to bake, and based on the look on his face, he was quite serious.

But the best one was the foreman of the group, who told Lila seeing her sweet face made him diabetic, so she owed it to him to come back soon to make sure he hadn't died or something.

"What is the perfume you are wearing, Lila, that gets these fellows all worked up? You're like a bee with honey." Amelia laughed.

"You know what I'm wearing? I'm wearing the scent 'unreachable.' I find more guys trying to get my attention now than I did when I was in my twenties. I blame it on the fact that I don't want any of them. My mother used to say treat them like dogs and they'll always come back for more. How right she was."

"But you don't treat Rusty that way." Amelia played devil's advocate.

"No." Lila tilted her head to the left. The fact that she didn't say another word made Amelia smile. Just as she was about to pressure her friend for more information, her phone went off.

"Let me guess." Lila pulled out the morning's receipts to work on. "John?"

"What tipped you off?" Amelia groaned.

"The red color that took over your cheeks."

"Hi, John." Amelia pinched her face as if the phone had suddenly transformed into a dirty sock or block of Limburger cheese that she didn't want close to her.

"Amelia. What is this that the kids don't want to go to the reception?"

Amelia shrugged. "What do you want from me, John? You left a voicemail for your son, sacking him from the role of best man. You didn't even tell him in person. What do you expect them to do?"

"You need to fix this, Amelia."

"Me?" She clenched the phone in a death grip. "No."

"Amelia, how is it going to look if my own kids aren't at the reception?"

"John, what did you think was going to happen? Did you think they were going to just say, 'Oh, okay, Dad. Cool. Whatever you and Jennifer want.' Is that really what you thought would happen? Your children are growing up with or without you. They are both old enough to decide how they want to proceed with what was a raw deal from their father."

"Amelia. It's my wedding."

"Who's the bride here, John, you or Jennifer? I know it's your wedding. Which is why you should have stuck up for your kids." Amelia could tell John was trying to think of a rebuttal. In his universe, this should have been accepted without question.

"Maybe they shouldn't come at all."

Amelia felt like she'd been punched in her gut. "I'm *not* telling them that," she spat. "You don't mean it. I know you're trying to make Jennifer happy because she's probably freaking out over flowers and napkins. But these are your children. They aren't me. Don't beat them up over this."

"What the hell is that supposed to mean?" John stammered.

Amelia let out a deep breath. "Let the kids do what they want, John. You know they'll look beautiful. They'll behave. And if they want to leave after the ceremony, then you make sure they get in a cab and have cab fare." *Because I'm not paying a sixty-dollar cab ride from your freakish ceremony at Agate Beach in Portland,* the little devil on her left shoulder snickered.

"I've got another call, Amelia. I have to take this." John's voice sounded defeated. Amelia didn't care. She tapped the red button that disconnected the call. Her lips stuck out as she thought for a moment and felt her boiling blood reduce to a simmer.

"You okay?" Lila asked carefully.

"Yes, I'm fine," Amelia said as if she were quoting gospel. "My kids are fine. Better than fine. They are wonderful. But their dad… I think he's starting to forget that." She clenched her fists.

"Well, there may not be anything you can do about that," Lila replied.

"I know."

Before Amelia could continue, she saw Joyce Ross come out of the revolving door and link her arm through that of a man Amelia thought was very familiar.

As she watched, Joyce was talking earnestly to the man. He appeared to be half listening when he looked at Amelia, smiled, and waved. "Amelia!" he called to her as he quickened his step, slipping out of Joyce's grasp and approaching the truck.

Amelia snapped her fingers. "Mike!" She smiled and reached her hand out the service window to shake his. "I knew you looked familiar but couldn't place it until I heard your voice. How in the world are you?"

"Fine. Just fine. I don't think you ever met my wife, Joyce."

"Awkward." Lila coughed.

"Only from buying a couple of my cupcakes. It's nice to meet you, Joyce." Amelia extended her hand, but Joyce merely looked at it. She gave Amelia that same *don't really like you* flash of a smile.

"How do you know my husband?" It sounded like a loaded question.

"My ex-husband plays softball with your husband," Amelia said carefully.

"I never got a chance to tell you that I'm really sorry things with you and John didn't work out," Mike added.

"Well, no use complaining." Amelia shrugged. "No one will listen."

Mike chuckled. Joyce looked at her watch.

"This is my partner in cupcakes, Lila Bergman."

"How are you?" Lila reached her hand out of the window and gave Mike's hand a hearty couple of pumps. She didn't let Joyce have a chance to leave her hanging.

"We see everybody coming and going with the truck parked here. We've not seen you before, Mike. You guys heading off to something exciting in the neighborhood?" Lila asked smoothly.

"Dinner," Joyce interrupted. "And if we don't get going, we'll be late."

Mike looked at his watch. His expression didn't change, but instead he blinked quickly, looked at the sidewalk, then gathered up a smile from way down deep and looked at Amelia. "I guess we better get going." Amelia thought of Adam telling his friends he couldn't go out with them after he was caught with fireworks in his backpack. Mike sounded exactly like that.

"Well, it was really nice seeing you again, Mike." Amelia smiled. "And it was nice meeting you, Joyce." Again, Amelia got that nasty flash of a grin before Joyce turned and began walking without Mike.

"Take care, Amelia. Lila, it was nice to meet you." Mike waved as he shuffled off to catch up with his wife.

"Now that's an odd couple." Lila watched with one drawn-on red eyebrow arched high up on her forehead. "You didn't know that woman was his wife?"

"When Christine said 'Ross,' it didn't even click. I mean, it's a pretty common name."

Lila nodded at Amelia.

"But she never went to any of the softball

games. I only went to a few every season because, well, they were boring. But I had to make an appearance, you know. How it would look and all." Amelia rolled her eyes at the bad memory of her marriage. "But I never saw her there. I'd have remembered."

CHAPTER FOURTEEN

ON HER WAY HOME, Amelia wondered why Joyce Ross was so standoffish.

"Maybe she just doesn't like you, Amelia," she said to herself. "It is possible that not everyone will like you when they meet you." She chuckled and continued talking to herself. "I wonder if she told Mike about our caged free eggs and the call to the Department of Agriculture and all that nonsense?" She frowned. "Probably not. From the looks of it, he was probably better off not saying anything even if she did tell him all about it."

While waiting at a red light four blocks from home,

Amelia's cell phone went off in her pocket. She didn't recognize the number, but something told her to answer the call.

"Is this Amelia Harley?" The voice was that of a young woman.

"Yes. This is she."

"Hi, Amelia. This is Vivika Korseky. I'm returning your call."

Amelia nearly dropped the phone. With all the excitement with John and the wedding and the kids, she had forgotten all about leaving her a message. "Oh, yes. Hi, Vivika. Thank you so much for returning my call."

"I read about the murder in the paper. Have they arrested Joyce Ross yet?"

"What?" Amelia was surprised at Vivika's bluntness. "Why would you say that?"

"I worked at Master Ketchup for eight months, right? Now, I'm no Girl Friday, but let's face it, secretarial work isn't brain surgery. They fired me because Joyce Ross is crazy." Amelia heard Vivika take a sip of something on the other line. If the woman were drunk, this conversation would make a lot more sense. "And they'd rather appease that lunatic than fire her. Are you hearing me?"

"Vivika, I'm sorry, but I don't quite follow."

"I'll bet you don't." She chuckled. "Make yourself comfortable and pour yourself a cup of tea, sweetheart, because I've got some stories for you. And your friend Christine—check with her on all of them if you don't believe me."

Amelia did make herself comfortable as she quickly got home, pulled into the driveway, shut off the engine, and sat in the truck with the phone to her ear.

"So, like I said, I worked at Master Ketchup for around eight months. Within the first week I was warned about Joyce."

"Warned?" Amelia asked.

"The other secretaries told me that she had the tendency to mention personal things about herself that were inappropriate under the best of circumstances."

"Can I ask like what?"

"You can," Vivika said. "I'll only tell you what she told me. Let's see, she told me she had been molested when she was four. Nice, right? She was raped when she was fifteen. Of course she was. She had breast cancer. Then she had lupus. The reason she and Mike had no children was because Mike had E.D. But then she said she didn't want children to add to the misery of the world. Overpopulation and all." Vivika took another sip of whatever she was drinking. "Yes, and Mike also suffered from recurring jock itch. He had several affairs. He had contracted an STD."

"She told *you* all of this?"

"This was after I'd only been there about six weeks!" Vivika chuckled. "It's crazy, right? So, she gets a hold of herself or something, and the next thing I know she's switched gears. Now, she wants me to share. *Quid pro quo*, Clarice. Like that *Silence of the Lambs* movie, right?"

"Why do you think she wanted you to tell her about your past?"

"At first I really thought that she may have felt bad that she was constantly chatting me up and didn't ask me anything about myself. So I really thought she was trying to be nice."

"But she wasn't?"

"Ha! I didn't have any sob stories like she did. Let me just say I don't believe the lot of them, okay? Either she's making all that up, or she is the unluckiest woman to ever walk God's earth. You feel me?"

"So what happened?"

"Well, as I got to know some of the other girls I started comparing notes. She's telling one girl she was molested when she was ten. To still another, she said she had fibromyalgia. I think Lyme disease was thrown in there. She told another girl her parents died on that bridge where people claimed to see the Mothman. Right? You still with me on this?"

Amelia's head was spinning. "So, let me ask you about what I heard."

"I can hardly wait," Vivika chirped. "Let me have it."

"I heard you gave her husband a book on motorcycles and that got you fired."

"Really?" Vivika chuckled, and Amelia was sure she could hear her shaking her head. "Mike Ross has a Harley-Davidson motorcycle that apparently is like his second wife. Joyce hates it."

"Do you know why?"

"Sure. She told me Mike cracked his head on the street in a motorcycle accident about two decades ago. He was in the hospital for six months. She thought he was going to die. He had a near-death experience. *She* had a near-death experience. But alas, he would not heed the warning their combined near-death experiences offered, and still rode without a helmet."

Amelia sat still. She wasn't sure what to say.

"Some bad luck, right?"

"I'll say," Amelia concurred.

"So, by this time I was starting to call bullshit on her stories. Excuse my language. I'm crude at times. But this whole ordeal gets me fired up."

"I can imagine," Amelia added.

"So, whenever Joyce would approach me with a new fantasy to share, like she was going to the doctor because she was afraid her uterine cyst had returned, I'd say I was going to the doctor for a lump under my arm. She said Mike was battling with depression? I said my uncle had a goiter. Was it childish? Sure. Was it fun? Absolutely! But, I flew too close to the sun.

"I had a book on motorcycles that I had picked up several years ago. I liked the pictures, and I draw in my spare time, so it was just a reference book for me to practice with. Rather than throw it away, I waltzed into Mike's office and offered it to him. You would have thought I offered the guy a golden ticket to Willy Wonka's chocolate factory. He was really grateful. So I asked him about his accident."

There was a pause. Amelia could tell that, for as much as Vivika may have been enjoying razzing Joyce, this part of the story bothered her. Amelia knew what was coming, and it bothered her, too.

"He wasn't in an accident. Never was. No one

he knew was ever in a motorcycle accident." She cleared her throat. "I apologized and said it must have been one of the other guys. I said I must have heard it wrong. But I could tell by the look on his face that he knew where I had gotten the idea."

"Then what?" Amelia's voice was soft and motherly.

"Take a guess." Vivika chortled. "Security showed up at my desk. In front of everyone, Joyce told me to pack up my desk, and I was escorted out. The end. They didn't try and fight my unemployment. So at least there was that."

Amelia shook her head and let out a sigh.

"That's it in a nutshell, Amelia. I'll bet if you asked around, you might find a few other stories, ailments, diseases, loss of limbs that grew back, and I'm sure there's an alien abduction in there somewhere." Vivika laughed. "You probably think I'm cruel because I make fun of this."

"I don't know you, Vivika. I can only imagine how it felt to be in this position at work. I'm not sure how I'd have reacted if it were me."

"Truthfully, I don't know who is more of a crackpot, Joyce Ross or the staff that keeps her on board. I'm glad to be out of that lunatic asylum.

Getting fired was anything but the end of the world."

"I'm glad you landed on your feet, Vivika," Amelia said sincerely. "I appreciate your calling me. Can I give you a call again if I have a question?"

"Sure. I enjoy badmouthing that place. If I could get paid for that, I'd be a rich woman." She chuckled.

"Thanks, Vivika."

"Take care, Amelia. Good luck."

Once inside the house, Amelia heard the kids talking upstairs.

"Hello!" she yelled to them as she dropped her purse on the floor.

"Hi, Mom!" they yelled in unison.

Both of them together in Meg's room? Those kids are planning something, Amelia thought, but proceeded into the kitchen. Whatever it was, she'd worry about it later. Her conversation with Vivika left her exhausted.

It all sounded strange, but Joyce Ross's behavior, if what Vivika said was true, was not murderous. *Was it?* Amelia could remember girls she knew in high school who bragged about hanging out with rock stars or famous actors, and everyone knew there was no truth to it at all.

One girl insisted the band Guns n' Roses came to her house to party with her on weekends. Utter nonsense! But that didn't stop her from continuing to talk as if it were gospel truth. It was a cry for help, maybe. But not a motive to kill.

Now, an ex-husband that doesn't invite his children to his wedding was another story. That might be considered a motive to kill.

No matter what was going on with Master Ketchup, Amelia's stomach was in knots after her conversation with John. She waited to see if he'd called the kids before bringing it up to them. There was no way she was going to breathe a word of his idiotic idea unless she had to.

CHAPTER FIFTEEN

"THANK GOODNESS IT'S FRIDAY," Amelia mumbled while rubbing her head. "I was up half the night. I'm worried about this wedding business. My dreams were all jumbled up. Now I've got a screaming headache, and we're out of aspirin."

"You poor thing," Lila said soothingly, handing Amelia a bottle of water. "There is a drugstore about two blocks from here. We aren't officially open yet. Why don't you take a walk? The change in scenery will do you good, and a little cardio can't hurt."

"I think I will, Lila. Thankfully it's a cloudy day or the sun would just burn me." Amelia grabbed her purse and hopped off the truck. "I'll be back in ten."

"I'll hold down the fort." Lila winked.

As Amelia started walking in the direction of the Walgreens drugstore, she thought that maybe she'd pick up a nice-smelling soap or some lotion for Lila. Where would she be without her? Still struggling and probably missing several thousand dollars due to bad bookkeeping, that's where she'd be.

It would be nice to get back to Food Truck Alley, too. That was where her cupcake business started, and she missed seeing all the familiar faces, not to mention the smells from Gavin's Philly cheesesteak truck and Charming Wok's Chinese, mixed with the freshly cut grass of the dining area.

Still, business was surprisingly good. Great, in fact, regardless of the rumbling trucks that shook the street as they roared by.

Not to mention you got to see your best friend every day for a week. Amelia smiled. Seeing Christine was great, even if it was just to chat for a few minutes in between work. *But I don't think I helped solve Danielle Wilcox's murder, and unfortunately it looks like Dan apprehended the right guy, no matter how much Christine liked him.*

She shook her head and shrugged as she talked to herself. When she got to Walgreens and stepped through the automatic doors, she was too wrapped up in her own thoughts to hear the dispute happening at the pharmacist's desk at the back of the shop.

First, she meandered down the soap and lotion aisle. A pretty purple box with red and pink flowers on it caught her eye. Holding it to her nose, Amelia inhaled the sweet smell of lavender and cherry blossom.

I might get this for myself, too, she thought as she scanned for a matching body lotion.

"I called the prescription in yesterday!" A loud female voice boomed down the aisles. "This is completely unacceptable!"

"Ma'am, I'm sorry," came a calmer male voice, "but the prescription didn't come in until after five o'clock."

"That is not my problem!" The woman shouted. "I'll have you know that my husband has direct contact with the chairman of the Food and Drug Administration!" Amelia thought that woman's tone sounded familiar.

"That's fine, ma'am, but even he can't change the fact that your prescription came in after five," the pharmacist said.

"I will have you and your pharmacy reported to

the FDA! They'll investigate why you are with-holding medications from patients who have ordered them, and—"

"Ma'am, we aren't withholding your medica-tion. It just isn't here yet. We will have your prescription filled by noon," the pharmacist replied. Amelia clutched the soap and lotion to her as she slowly walked to the end of the aisle and peeked to her right, toward the pharmacy. "All you have to do is come back and…"

"Oh, I'll be back, all right! I know what you're doing! And I know who you are! Don't think I don't!"

Amelia gulped as she stared.

"Well, my husband will be very interested to know how you people are handling things here!" she bellowed. "Don't be surprised when the news crews show up and ask what you're doing with the patients' medications!"

"Joyce?" Amelia called to her. Joyce's head snapped in Amelia's direction like a woman possessed. "Is… everything okay?" Amelia hoped a familiar face and a calm voice might bring Joyce back from the edge, but it seemed to have the oppo-site effect.

With that same sinister flash of smile, Joyce

pointed at Amelia then turned on her heel and stomped out of the pharmacy, leaving the employees and a couple of patrons to hem and haw over the spectacle.

Even though her headache had disappeared, Amelia grabbed a bottle of aspirin, added it to her fancy soap and bottle of lotion, quickly paid, and then rushed to the Pink Cupcake.

When she got there, only Lila was at the truck. A few last-minute stragglers were hurrying into the building to beat the bell. Everything looked normal.

"What in the world happened to you?" Lila asked, squinting. "You look like the devil chased you all the way here."

"You won't believe who was at the drugstore making a big, huge fuss." Amelia pulled out her phone and dialed Christine's number.

"Hey, girl," Christine whispered. "I'm supposed to be heading into a meeting in a few. What's up?"

"Joyce Ross. She ever tell you stories about being ill or having some kind of disease?" Amelia asked while looking at Lila.

"I try to avoid her. But I've heard people say she has a wide range of ailments. Not sure what that means, but it seems like once one thing clears up she's got something new," Christine replied.

"I think there is something wrong with her, and I'm sure that there is more to this than anyone thought." Just as Amelia was about to relay the incident she witnessed at the pharmacy, she looked up to see Joyce standing in the doorway at the back of the truck.

"Joyce." Amelia still had the phone to her mouth. "I'm sorry, Joyce, but you aren't allowed on my truck. It's not a personal thing. It's a safety code."

"Oh my... is she on your truck?" Christine gasped.

"You and I need to have a talk," Joyce hissed.

CHAPTER SIXTEEN

"WHAT DID SHE SAY?" Christine asked. "What's going on? Do you need me down there?"

"Yes." Amelia said, answering Christine while appeasing Joyce. "I need you to step off the truck, Joyce."

"You heard what the boss said." Lila stepped up. She was like a mama bear. "Please, step off the truck."

Joyce turned and walked down the metal steps, but she wasn't going to go peacefully. A second later came a whopping bang that echoed through the interior of the truck.

"What?"

"She hit the truck." Lila gasped.

Bang! Bang! Bang!

"I need to talk to you!" Joyce screamed.

Before Amelia could stop her, Lila went stomping down the steps. "Now you just wait one minute!" she shouted, marching up to Joyce. "You can't take out your issues on our truck! That is vandalism! And I may not know the director of the Department of Agriculture, but I know Officer Friendly, and I've got his number memorized. Now if you want to talk…"

Lila tried to lay down the law with a woman who was not too interested in being reasonable. She smiled at Lila, jerked her chin at her, batted her eyes at her and waved her hands like she was putting some kind of curse on her.

As Amelia stepped off the truck, Lila turned and Joyce pushed her out of the way to tower over Amelia.

Lila staggered and lost her balance, falling to the ground just as Christine, Mike Ross, and a member of security sprinted out of the building.

"Joyce!" Amelia put her hands up defensively. "It's okay! Really, it is!"

"No! You don't understand!" Joyce yelled. "You have no idea what is going to happen now. Those people, they did this to me before. They say they didn't get my prescription, but they did. They are holding out on me because they know it makes me sick."

"Do you think that's what they're doing?" Amelia played along as she inched closer to Joyce.

Joyce's face became stone serious. "It is what they're doing." Her voice trembled. "They're doing it on purpose so things will get messed up again."

"I'll bet they are," Amelia concurred. She looked to Mike, who stared at his wife but obviously didn't want to get any closer than he already was. "No one listens, though, do they?"

"No!" Joyce barked. "They think I'm making it all up! But I know it's true!"

"You know what's true, Joyce."

Joyce started to sway on her feet. She took a step back and stared at Amelia. "They're putting something in my pills. It's not the medicine it's supposed to be. They want me sick so I'll do things like I did before." Her eyes filled with tears.

"It's okay, Joyce." Amelia stared as this woman, who was built like an Olympic swimmer, began to crumble and break apart before her eyes.

Christine ran to Lila's side and quickly helped her up. The side of her blue jeans had a tear in them, and her palms were black with red scratches.

"Don't say anything, Joyce!" Mike ordered. "It's okay. You don't need to say anything more."

Sirens could be heard coming from a few blocks away.

"You're just tired, Joyce," Mike said. "You don't know what you're saying. She's tired. Her medication has been a mess and…"

Amelia reached her hand out to Joyce and gently put her hand on her arm. Joyce's skin was ice cold to the touch.

It was as if she had found a moment of clarity. Amelia looked into Joyce's eyes and watched them focus on her face. She saw a hint of recognition and then a deep sadness, which probably filled her whole body all the way to her feet. "I killed her," Joyce whispered with trembling lips.

"No, Joyce!" Mike yelled.

"I can't keep this inside me anymore. They're letting it eat me up from the inside out," she confided to Amelia.

"Who is?"

"The people who give me my medicine. They wanted to see if I could be trusted. I guess I can't." She started to sob, but after a moment, when the police cars screeched to a stop and two uniformed officers and Detective Dan Walishovsky and his partner, Eugene, appeared, Joyce looked at Amelia again. "I'm so sorry."

Amelia looked to Dan and nodded.

An ambulance pulled up seconds later, and the double doors at the back of the van popped open. Two EMTs hopped out with a stretcher in tow.

"I don't think she'll hurt anyone," Amelia said. She kept Joyce at arm's length, but the woman made no attempt to fight or resist Dan, who escorted her to the back of the ambulance.

"Mike?" Amelia looked at him with narrow eyes.

Mike thrust his hands in his pockets and stepped up to Amelia.

"She was diagnosed with depression. Something happened, and she needed a little boost so…"

"What happened?"

Mike rubbed the back of his neck and looked around.

"I had an affair. It didn't mean anything. It was just one time and…"

"With Danielle?"

"No. I never told Joyce who because there was no need. It was over." He swallowed hard and looked over to the ambulance, where Joyce had been loaded up and Dan was patiently talking to her. Lila and Christine were giving Eugene their versions of what they saw to the uniformed officers. "But she *thought* it was Danielle. She thought it was the waitress at the restaurant we went to last night. She thought it was the woman who cuts my hair. She thought it was one of the girls on the softball team. She thought it was you. It didn't matter what I said. The medication she was taking made her see things. Hear things. I thought it would be just a matter of time before her body got used to it or she changed her prescription and everything went back to normal."

"So you knew she killed Danielle, and you didn't—"

"Hold on a minute!" he shouted, pointing a shaking finger in Amelia's face. "I didn't know anything. I had my suspicions, but I didn't know for sure. I mean, when she's threatened to kill half the females in the city, it's hard to believe she was responsible for this one. Right?"

"And what about Charles Howe? The guy the police have in custody for Danielle's murder? Were you just going to let that go?"

"N-n-no!" Mike stuttered. "Of course not." He nodded and shifted from one foot to the other. "I would have said something."

"When?" Amelia hated to sound so petty, but she could see why John and Mike had gotten along. *What a piece of work.*

"Look. I don't have to answer to you, okay?" Mike pushed his hair back from his forehead. "I'm going to be with my wife. Excuse me."

Mike hustled over to the back of the ambulance and quickly spoke with Dan without turning around and looking at any of the people in the small crowd that had gathered.

Amelia hurried up to Lila. "Lila, why did you try and get in that woman's way?" She pushed a stray flaming-red wisp away from her friend's eye. "Are you all right?"

"I'm fine." Lila shook her head. "I think I've been hanging out at Rusty's place too much. Starting to think I can run with the big dogs when I really should be sittin' on the porch."

"Why don't you come inside the building, and I'll get some antiseptic on those scratches," Christine offered.

"Yeah, good idea. Thanks, Chris," Amelia replied.

As her friends walked off, yacking like a couple of old friends, Amelia turned to see Dan approaching. A paramedic slammed the ambulance's doors shut, and within seconds the vehicle made a U-turn, lights flashing and sirens blaring as they hurried Joyce to the emergency room.

"What do you think?" Amelia took a deep breath and folded her arms over her chest.

"From the little bit I got out of Mrs. Ross, I'm afraid that a mixture of drugs for depression and anxiety with conflicting side effects and question-able dosages caused her to become violent. She killed Danielle Wilcox. That's for sure. But I can't say there was malicious intent. Had she not been on those drugs, I think that girl would still be alive today."

"That's sad." Amelia huffed. "What about her husband? Did he say anything to you?"

"He didn't have to." Dan rocked on his heels and rubbed his chin. "He thinks I don't know a guilty conscience when I see one. We'll be having a good, long heart-to-heart at the station once Joyce is stabilized."

"What are they going to do with her?"

"Well, first they have to wean her off the poisons she was on. According to her and her husband, she's been mixing and matching her prescriptions for almost eighteen months." Dan looked at the ground.

"That explains the stories I heard about her complaining about weird ailments and accidents that never happened." Amelia looked at the sky. "She was probably hallucinating or thinking her dreams were real."

"The doctors will have to find a new combination of drugs that keep her stitched up along the sides," Dan continued. "After they get her regulated and stabilized, they will decide if she's fit to stand trial. She'll be in an institution before they transfer her to jail."

"What a mess." Amelia slipped her hand into Dan's. "It's so easy to think the person responsible for Danielle's death had horns or fangs or just a black, rotten heart. But that isn't that woman they just sped away with."

"No, it's not." Dan squeezed her hand. "But I'm afraid she's going to have to answer for herself, nonetheless."

"Right." Amelia shrugged. "You know, there isn't a real clear-cut bright side to this situation. But you know they don't have any children. That's a blessing in disguise if I ever heard one. Not to be morbid or anything."

"Speaking of children." Dan looked at Amelia

with worry on his face. "How are your kids doing? Any change in the whole wedding drama?"

She didn't tell Dan about John's brilliant idea that the kids not attend at all. She was afraid John might come out of the church with his new bride in tow only to find a big yellow boot on their limo.

"They've decided to handle things themselves."

"Is that a good thing, or will I be getting a phone call at three in the morning to bail them out of the pokey?"

Amelia laughed. "No. I'm pretty confident they will handle it with tact. Something their father should have done."

"I'll be interested to see how it turns out."

"That makes two of us." Amelia smiled when she saw the slight smirk on Dan's face.

"I'll keep bail money ready anyway."

"Well, just in case. Better safe than sorry."

"That's right." Dan slipped his arm around Amelia and kissed the top of her head as he walked her back to the Pink Cupcake.

CHAPTER SEVENTEEN

"CAN'T you savages see I'm on the phone!" Christine yelled, making Amelia hold her phone away from her ear. "Why do we just have a glass of wine together over the telephone when we both really need those boxes of wine from the grocery store? One apiece."

"Just a box of wine and a long straw." Amelia giggled. "Hey, you just gave me an idea."

"Wait. If you're thinking what I'm thinking…"

"What are you thinking?"

"An alcoholic cupcake?"

"It's like we share the same brain!" Amelia laughed. "But not wine. Something a little more elegant."

"Right, like Old Style or Coors?" Christine chuckled.

Neither woman had finished her first glass of wine, but they'd laughed almost continuously since they got on the phone with each other half an hour before.

"That would be a challenge," Amelia concurred. "But I was thinking more like a White Russian, or maybe a Bailey's and coffee."

"Bailey's and coffee cupcake. Oh my gosh. I can taste that right now. With a frosting…"

"Yes. A frosting that's just a little bitter, like maybe a cream cheese base or something." Amelia smiled. "Oh, thank you, Christine. I'm over my creative block, and I owe it to you. Just a few minutes on the phone, and it's like a miracle just happened."

"Please tell me you're going to come back to the factory once or twice a month. It was so awesome getting to see you every day. I'm going to miss that."

"Me, too. Hey, has Charles Howe come back to work?"

"No." Christine's voice was heavy. "Once he was released from the jail, he came back to the office, cleared out his things, and quit. I guess it was a little too hard for him to face everyone. People would be asking if he was okay and what happened in the jail and all kinds of weird things people always want to know."

"You're probably right." Amelia shook her head. "It might just be me, but it sounds like he really loved Danielle. Maybe it was like a sister. Maybe more. But I can understand how he feels. Too many memories."

"Yeah. I meant to tell you that Penny is doing better, too. That poor thing was carrying the weight of the world on her scrawny little bony shoulders."

"Nice description, Chris."

"Well, it's true." Amelia heard her take a sip of her wine, so she did the same. "Human Resources got her a therapist. And, in typical corporate style, they offered counseling and therapy dogs to anyone who was feeling particularly affected by the events over the past week."

"You going?" Amelia snickered.

"I would. They put a chaise lounge in the human resources waiting room. But no. I'm not freaking out about this. I had you there. My girl, watchin' my back."

"That's right."

Just as Amelia was going to ask Christine if she

had heard any more about Joyce Ross, her front door opened.

"Hold on, Chris. I think the kids are home from the wedding."

Adam and Meg came in the house, laughing and talking.

"Hey! How'd it go?"

"It was fine. The ceremony was boring, but I made sure everyone signed the guest book. I even hunted them down in their seats and in the parking lot," Adam boasted.

"Well, good for you. They'll be happy you did that even if you were pushy." Amelia smiled. "How about you? Did you have fun?" She looked at her daughter.

"It was okay. Dad looked nice. Jennifer looked pretty. But those gold lamé bridesmaids' dresses were so bright on the beach, it was like they were shining a mirror right in the eyes of all their guests." Meg giggled.

"It sounds like you guys were having a good time. You still didn't want to stay for the reception?" Amelia was surprised. She knew Adam had been hurt. John didn't make any attempt to rectify the situation. But the kids didn't act like anything was amiss.

"No," Adam stated. "Meg and I had a long talk, and we decided it was Dad's special day. We'd go and do what we were told, and then we'd leave so he wouldn't have to feel funny and neither would we."

"Well, that is very mature of you." Amelia beamed. "Did you hear that, Chris? You hear how my kids handled things with class?"

"Besides. A lady always knows when to leave." Meg waved a white-gloved hand. She'd insisted on a burgundy-colored dress she had seen at a thrift store, which reminded her of a dress June Allyson wore in *Little Women,* except it was just a little past her knees and didn't require a petticoat. She even wore a net to make her long hair fold up prettily along her neck.

"I've got to get out of this tux," Adam complained. "I'm not wearing one of these when I get married." He pulled at the cummerbund and unbuttoned his collar.

"Who'd marry you? Godzilla isn't real," Meg teased as she turned on her heel and went upstairs.

"Funny." Adam rolled his eyes and retreated to the basement door. "Mom, can I go to Amy's? I told her I'd be home early."

"You can." Amelia smiled. "Why don't you go

over there in your tux? You look very handsome. Give her your corsage."

Adam smiled broadly and nodded. In a flash, the front door opened and slammed shut.

"Can you believe it? And I was up night after night worrying about them," Amelia whispered to Christine.

"I'm really impressed," Christine added. "I mean, I'm impressed when my own kids don't eat paste for two days in a row. So maybe I'm not the person to listen to. But this whole wedding situation, well, it brought the worst out of John. But it brought the best out of Adam and Meg. It really did."

"I hope John stabilizes once the honeymoon is over." Amelia wished. "I just hope he comes back to the kids. I hope he sees them not just with his eyes but with his heart."

"I hope he does, too," Christine chimed in. "But love is blind. Especially in gold lamé."

RECIPE 1: DARK CHOCOLATE AND BACON CUPCAKE

makes 24

Ingredients:

- 12 slices bacon
- 2 cups all-purpose flour
- 2 cups white sugar
- 2 eggs
- 1 cup cold, strong, brewed coffee
- 1 cup buttermilk
- 1/2 cup vegetable oil
- 3/4 cup unsweetened cocoa powder & 1 tbsp for dusting
- 2 tsp baking soda
- 1 tsp baking powder
- 1/2 teaspoon sea salt

Chocolate Frosting:
- 2 3/4 cups icing sugar
- 6 tbsp unsweetened cocoa powder
- 6 tbsp butter
- 5 tbsp evaporated milk
- 1 tsp vanilla extract

Preheat oven to 375 degrees F. Line 24 muffin tins. Cook bacon in skillet over medium-high heat. Drain and set aside.

In a bowl, add flour, sugar, 3/4 cup cocoa powder, baking soda, baking powder, and sea salt. Mix. Make a well in the center and pour in eggs, coffee, buttermilk, and vegetable oil. Stir until blended. Crumble bacon and add 3/4, leaving the rest for garnish.

Divide the batter into lined cups. Bake for 20-25 minutes, until the top springs back when lightly pressed. Let cool.

To make frosting, sift icing sugar and cocoa into a bowl. In a bigger bowl, cream butter until smooth, gradually beating in sugar mixture alternately with milk. Lastly, blend in vanilla. Cream until light and fluffy.

When cupcakes are cool, frost with chocolate frosting. Sprinkle bacon crumbles on top, and dust with cocoa powder.

RECIPE 2: APPLE PIE CRUMBLE CUPCAKE

makes 24

Ingredients:
- 2 apples, peeled and chopped
- 3 eggs
- 2 cups graham cracker crumbs
- 1 cup water
- 1 package yellow cake mix
- 1/2 cup vegetable oil
- 1 tsp ground cinnamon
- 1/2 tsp nutmeg
- 1/4 cup melted butter

Preheat oven to 325 degrees F. Line 24 muffin cups.

Put chopped apples in a food processor, mince, and then transfer to a bowl.

In a separate bowl, beat together cake mix, eggs, water, and vegetable oil with an electric mixer until smooth. Fold apple mixture into the batter.

In another bowl, pour in graham cracker crumbs, cinnamon, and nutmeg. Add melted butter and mix with your hands until crumbs are moist. Fill each liner with 1 teaspoon of crumb mixture. Top with batter. Sprinkle any remaining crumbs on top.

Bake for 15 minutes, or until a toothpick comes out clean. Let cool in tin before removing.

Harper Lin is the *USA TODAY* bestselling author of 6 cozy mystery series including *The Patisserie Mysteries* and *The Cape Bay Cafe Mysteries*.

When she's not reading or writing mysteries, she loves going to yoga classes, hiking, and hanging out with her family and friends.

www.HarperLin.com

www.ingramcontent.com/pod-product-compliance
Lightning Source LLC
Chambersburg PA
CBHW050852180626
46814CB00007B/2740